FASHIONABLE
Desires

Carol Fike

The Reading Glass
BOOKS

The Reading Glass Books
(888) 420-3050
production@readingglassbooks.com

Chapter 1

It was in the middle of summer, and it was a typical hot humid day. Tiffany Long was lying in the hot summer sun, in the nude, as she liked to feel the sun beating down on her naked body. She was tanned and dark brown and had beads of sweat pouring out all over her body. She was a very tall young woman. She stood five feet, ten inches, and when she wore heels, she was extremely tall.

She had gorgeous, long blond hair which she had tied up in a bun.

She was a model at a nearby photography studio and absolutely loved what she did for a living.

She had been in the modeling business since she had gotten out of high school at age seventeen.

She graduated from college earlier the same summer, and she was a very intelligent woman to say the least. She was almost a straight A student.

She had a very pretty face, and the one trait that stood out about her most was her pretty blue eyes. She was a strikingly beautiful girl, a one-in-a-million girl, if you saw her out you would recognize her if you were to see her again.

Any man would have gladly taken her out and shown her a good time.

Tiffany lived in her own private home, on the outskirts of San Francisco, California. Her commute to work was a busy one. She had grown up in that setting and that is where she intended to stay for the time being. She loved living life in the fast lane, so to speak.

She had an in-ground swimming pool which she used quite regularly.

Her home was very expensive and very attractively designed and elegant and it was also very unique.

She had a tile floor in her dining room, bathroom, and kitchen, and very expensive plush carpeting in the living room and bedroom. She had a pink tile floor in her bathroom, and in her dining room, she had a light blue color, as well as in the kitchen.

Her carpeting was light burgundy that was in the living room.

The kitchen was huge and had everything imaginable within it.

Tiffany was successful in many ways, but she had gotten a lot of help from her parents, who were very successful as well.

Her dad was an attorney, and her mom was a lawyer.

Tiffany had an older sister, Rachel, who was attractive as well, but unlike Tiffany, she had olive green eyes and auburn-colored hair. She had a younger brother Nick who was a very good-looking boy as well. Nick was a senior in high school. Both her sister and her brother were very successful as well.

As fate would have it, they all must have taken after their parents, David Gregory and Tracey Lynn Long.

None of the kids were married, but Rachel was dating a guy who was very successful and she had been going out with him for quite some time, and she thought he was about to ask her to marry him.

Rachel was a lawyer just like her mother and had been for a little over a year.

Nick, like his father, was going to college to be an attorney. He only had a couple more months until he graduated.

Nick had a couple girlfriends throughout his senior year but they just didn't last. He was a football player throughout school and a very good one at that. He did that as well as wrestling but football seemed to be his main sport of choice. He even considered playing football for a living after he graduated college. He is uncertain which route to take.

July fourth was the day after the next, and the kids' parents were throwing a big outing. David and Tracy invited several of their best friends.

The older people had mixed drinks, as David and Tracy had a bar in the one room of their house, and some of the people chose to just have beer.

They had an open fire where the people roasted hot dogs and marshmallows, and they had a buffet set up with all kinds of food.

It was quite a celebration and everyone was having a wonderful time.

Some of the women and men were in the huge pool David and Tracy owned. Tiffany and her best friends were lying in the hot summer sun talking, laughing at each other's jokes, and having a good time. The girls were drinking different kinds of mixed drinks.

Her friends' names were Jackie, Carrie, and Heather. All three of her friends had boyfriends and they were at the party also.

Her best friend Heather's boyfriend's name was Jason, and Heather and Jason together made a very attractive couple. They were engaged to be married in February the following year. They were getting married February fourteenth and Tiffany was picked to be the maid of honor. The other two girls were chosen to be bridesmaids.

Carrie had a one-year-old son to Eric and they weren't married yet; they were just living together. Their little boy looked a lot like Eric. Carrie's son was really a sweet little boy. They named him Mark and he had really **blond hair**. Her other friend Heather had just met Mike and the two of them were on and off all the time. They just didn't get along very well together.

The party lasted long into the night, and most of the people were talking and acting carefree as if they didn't have a worry in the world.

It turned out to be quite a party.

That night when Tiffany got home, she dressed, and climbed right into bed.

She figured on sleeping in the next day as it was Sunday and she usually slept in on Sundays.

Chapter 2

Sunday came and went quickly and Monday was here and Tiffany got up and showered, dressed and ate breakfast and was on her way to work, at six o'clock in the morning. As she entered the door to her place of work, she greeted Scott, her modeling agent. "Hello, Scott, How are you this morning?" Tiffany asked. "I'm wonderful. How are you?" "Oh, I'm doing better than I was yesterday morning. I woke up with a hangover. We had a big Fourth of July party and I over drank. I think most of the people there were drunk at the end of the day."

Tiffany had quite a day modeling clothes. She went up and down the runway so many times she felt like she could walk back and forth in her sleep, and she changed clothes numerous times. She was glad when the day was over and it was time to go home.

Although she liked many aspects of her job, she still had to look good all the time, and she had to wear high-heeled shoes, and they were killing her feet by the end of the day. She was happy to finally put on a comfortable pair of shoes.

The next day there was going to be a major fashion show, and Tiffany and all her friends she worked with were going to be in it.

"Well, I'll see you tomorrow early," Scott told Tiffany as she walked out the door.

"Yeah, it'll feel good to go home and relax before I go to bed," Tiffany said. "I need to get off my feet, they're killing me."

Tiffany stopped at a little sandwich shop and had a light supper. She always tried to eat light as when you were in the camera's eye, it showed every little pound that you gained.

That was one thing that was hard about her job and there were times she felt like indulging but she couldn't.

To be a fashion model, you had to exercise daily and Tiffany and the other girls all participated in an exercise program. That along with watching your calories all the time added up to how you looked.

Tiffany was around girls who absolutely starved themselves to look good. Some were anorexic, and they tried to hide the fact that they were, but they looked like skin and bones, at least that was what Tiffany thought.

Tiffany's one main complaint was that she loved chocolate, and if she even ate one candy bar, she had to work twice as hard after that so it wouldn't show on her.

Tiffany ate very light and she kind of picked at her food as she always did before a fashion show, as she wanted to look and be her best person she could be.

When she got home, it was seven o'clock at night. She checked her voicemail and she had a message from her mom first. "This is your mom, I just called to say hi, and see if everything is going well with you." She had another one from where she had placed an order, and one more from her sister.

"I'm getting out of these clothes and into the shower," she thought to herself.

The shower was relaxing to say the least and she had her robe on when the phone rang, and she picked it up and her mom was on the line.

"Hi, Tiffany," her mom said. "I just called to see if anything is new with you." Not much, Mom, since I talked to you the last time. We have a big fashion show tomorrow. Is there anything new as far as you're concerned?" she asked her mom. "No, not really, but they say no news is good news." "Yes, that is very true, Mom," Tiffany answered in reply.

"Well, I know you had a busy day, and it sounds like you'll have a busy day tomorrow, so I better let you go," Tracy told her daughter.

"Yeah, thanks for calling and thinking about me," Tiffany said.

"I love you, Mom!" "Yes, and I love you as much," Tracy said.

After getting off the phone to her mom, Tiffany turned on her big-screen TV. She turned all the lights off and turned down the TV and fell asleep.

She awoke the next day and it was early as usual when she got out of bed. She took her morning shower and dressed, ate breakfast, and got around to go to work.

Scott was there as usual, and when Tiffany walked through the door, Scott replied, "There's my star model." It wasn't like Tiffany to blush, but she did at that statement.

The girls all got ready as the fashion show was starting at nine o'clock. Everything went well up until eleven o'clock when Heather was walking out and she caught her high-heeled shoes on the carpet. She fell and screamed as she went down hard and almost fell off of the stage completely. Her friends and Scott all went to her rescue. "Are you hurt really badly?" They were all asking and wondering what they could do to help her.

"It's my ankle," she replied. "I think it's broken."

Scott asked to take her to the hospital to get a cast put on it. He went and called 911 and the ambulance was there within minutes. The driver and the paramedic loaded her onto a gurney and got her into the ambulance.

When they arrived at the hospital, they took her in and asked her a number of questions.

"We're going to take you and get your ankle x-rayed," the physician there told her.

She had Tiffany there with her and she said for her to call Jason and let him know what had happened.

After x-raying the right ankle, they told her it was badly broken. They put a cast on her ankle and told her not to be on it.

"We want the ankle to heel evenly," Dr. Donaldson told her.

"Well how long do I have to remain off it?" Heather asked.

"I would say four months at least. We will give you a set of crutches to use."

Jason came through the door and came over to comfort Heather.

"What happened, babe?" Jason asked her.

"Well we were putting on the fashion show and my high heels got caught on the carpet, and when I fell, I broke my ankle."

Jason bent to kiss her at that, and she felt a little better now that he was there to comfort her.

They brought her supper that night and breakfast the next morning. They kept her at the hospital for a week and then they told her she could go home, but the doctor told her to stay off the ankle as much as possible.

She was happy to be going home finally, and she was ready. Dr. Donaldson came back one last time and told her he was glad that it seemed to be healing quite well. Afterwards the nurse came in and they gave her instructions of what was expected of her.

Laura, her nurse, told her to make a follow-up appointment with her primary care physician and she also said that she wanted her to take a pain medicine and it would make her kind of sleepy and instructed her not to drive or do anything that would post further injury.

"We will call you back tomorrow to make sure you are doing well. Good luck to you. We wish you a very speedy recovery," and the two shook hands.

Afterwards they accommodated her with a wheelchair and took her out where Jason was waiting just outside the door.

"I guess I'm going to have to take care of you," Jason told her.

He took her home and helped her as much as he could by cooking her meals, cleaning, and doing the laundry.

"You're a pretty good cook and this is spoiling me," she added "Maybe I'll have to hire you."

"Oh no, this sounds scary," Jason told her.

The phone started ringing, and when Jason answered, it was Tiffany.

"Hello," Jason said.

Hi, Jason, can I talk to Heather?"

"You sure can," Jason said as he handed the phone to Heather.

Hi, Heather. I just called to say hello and I miss you at work."

"Yeah, I miss you too, and I wish I would be able to go to work. I'm afraid this incident is going to be hard on my figure, and I'll have to exercise twice as hard to get back in shape."

"I'll have to come over to your house and maybe we could go shopping together," Tiffany told Heather.

Yeah, that would be very nice as I haven't been able to go shopping for a while," Heather said.

"Scott said he might have to find a replacement for you, as we're really busy and we could use another girl."

Yeah, what a time for me to go getting hurt."

"Let's plan on going shopping on a Saturday. How about next Saturday?" Tiffany suggested.

"Sounds good to me," Heather replied. "I'm not doing anything else important."

"Well then Saturday it is," Tiffany said.

At that the two girls said their goodbyes.

Chapter 3

The next day it was business as usual at the modeling agency, and as Tiffany walked in the room, there were two new faces. Scott was getting the runway set up and showing the two new girls around. He was explaining to them what they had to do.

Tiffany learned that their names were Ashley and Mary Anne. Scott introduced the two new girls to Tiffany.

They were both very tall and they were attractive also.

Ashley had dark long elegant shiny hair and it hung halfway down her back. She was a very pretty girl and she was young. She was only nineteen. She was a freshman in college.

The other girl Mary Anne was a tall young girl with sandy blond hair and pretty green eyes. Her hair hung halfway down her back as well.

Both girls fared well and did a good job the first day.

All the girls got along well and had a good time together. They talked about everything from college to their likes and dislikes.

"Let's all go out tonight and have dinner," Tiffany suggested.

"Yeah, we're game for that," both Ashley and Mary Anne said.

As the girls were saying their goodbyes to Scott, he told them they all did an excellent job.

"I'll see you all tomorrow," Scott told them.

The girls walked down the street and talked to one another.

"Let's go to the little Tavern Inn," Ashley suggested.

"Sounds good to us," the girls agreed. The waitress asked what they wanted to drink as she handed them their menus.

They looked over their menus and they all picked out the baked codfish dinner with a baked potato and a salad.

They each had a mixed drink. They ate and talked and got along real well together.

The girls all thought they knew each other better by the end of the night.

As the girls all got into their vehicles, they said their goodbyes.

Mary Anne was a little too intoxicated as she had overdrank. She was going a little too fast and she hit a tree and the car rolled over and crushed her roof down and broke the window out. She was pinned inside the car, and as she laid there trapped inside, she wondered what was going to happen to her. She felt like her whole body was crushed and she was in severe pain.

There was a man coming up the road beside the car and she could see her car in his headlights; as he got a little closer, she could see by the way the car looked that whoever was inside would be lucky if they lived. He pulled over and called 911 and the ambulance and driver were there within minutes. The first thing they used was the jaws of life to get her out.

She didn't have a heartbeat at first and the paramedics tried to revive her. They worked together as fast as they could and had her breathing. They had her in the ambulance as quickly as possible.

She was hooked up to an IV, and as soon as they got her to the hospital, they did everything they could with their skilled hands as fast as they could work. She looked like a mummy by the time they had finished operating on her to stop the bleeding.

She was lying there on the hospital bed not knowing where she was. They were not certain, but they were hoping that they had saved her life.

They're getting there as fast as possible helped along with the fine surgeons who took care of her. The police found her purse and her ID was in it. Her name, the one policeman said, is Mary Anne London.

Well into the night she hung on and they watched her closely and kept an eye on her to make sure she was stable. She would still be lucky if she survives, they discussed between themselves. That night at the hospital was a trying one, but she was still with them in the morning. The nurse came in and changed her IV and said she was lucky just to be alive.

"She had a lot of broken bone," Dr. Bryan told some of the other doctors who were just starting there that day. "She has a concussion and we were unfortunately working hard, and we were working under a gun, so to speak."

"I wonder who her next of kin is?" the doctors asked each other.

"We found some pictures of her mom and dad in her bag, and she had three other pictures who must be her brothers and sister. We also found a picture of her. She is a beautiful girl. She looks like a model. We found some phone numbers and a few addresses." The doctors discussed this among themselves.

The police who were on duty called the numbers in her purse and went to the addresses listed as well. Their search was over around noon when they pulled up to the last address. As they knocked on the door, a woman came to the door and answered.

"Is this your daughter?" Police Officer Baker asked, as he showed her a picture.

"Yes, it is, is something wrong?" her mother asked with a look of concern.

"I'm afraid so, she had a very bad accident last night and she is in the San Bernardino Allegheny Hospital."

At that, her mother was in tears and her mom and dad were ready to go within minutes.

"You can follow us," the policeman said as they led them out of the driveway and to the hospital.

They were there within half an hour, and as the policemen led them into the room, her parents were absolutely ecstatic and her mother was still in shock as she looked at her daughter.

Her husband went out to talk to the two police officers and they explained everything.

The next day as the doctors made their rounds, they shook hands with Mary Anne's parents and told them her condition.

On her way to work the next day after the accident, Tiffany saw her friend's car all smashed up. Oh my god, she thought. I wonder if she survived or not.

At work, when she got there, Scott and the girls were talking about it as well, as they saw it on the news.

That sounds awful, they were telling one another.

"I saw her car as I was coming to work and it looked pretty bad."

She was in the private secluded room until four days later when she started to come around, and the first words she said were "I feel pain all over."

She could sense a feeling of her parents being near her.

She was finally in her own room in the hospital and she had improved a great deal and was talking to her parents, which was a very good sign.

That night after work, Tiffany drove over to the hospital to see her friend.

She couldn't hardly believe it was the same person she went out to dinner with only one week prior.

Tiffany talked to Mary Anne's mom and dad and she told them that night Mary Anne had her accident because she had been drinking a little too much.

Yeah, they said she was intoxicated and she was driving too fast, Mary Anne's mom told her.

Tiffany stayed for a while and afterwards Mary Anne's parents and Tiffany said their goodbyes.

After learning that Tiffany only met their daughter the day of the accident, both of Mary Anne's parents agreed that she was a really nice girl.

Mary Anne's parents went home that night as they wanted a break. They thought to themselves that they would be back the next day.

Tiffany went home that night, and as she climbed into bed, she was praying that Mary Anne would be better before too long.

Chapter 4

With the situation the way it was, Scott put an ad in the paper that he was hiring. He had a lot of girls that just didn't meet the qualifications to be a model. He had some who were either overweight or they weren't tall enough or they just didn't have the looks. Then he did have a select few in which to choose from.

After much consideration, he hired three girls.

Scott hired a very pretty girl from Texas, whose name was Star. She just graduated from college and she just previously won the Miss America contest. Star was a very intelligent girl. She had many awards from various things she had done thus far. Star was twenty-one years old and she had been dating a very good-looking man whose name was Justin. Justin was a star also, being that he was in many excellent movies, and he was very good and sufficient in what he did, how he looked, and everything about him spelled success.

The second girl he hired was also highly attractive, successful, and very confident. Her name was Jennifer and she was another very intelligent girl as well. She was a figure skater and an excellent skier. She was a straight A student. She was a freshman in college and she was nineteen. She also had a boyfriend who was very attractive and excellent at what he did.

The third girl, whose name was Samantha, was also very pretty and highly intelligent. She also was very upbeat and unique. She was a figure skater as well as a tennis player. She was twenty years old and she was a sophomore in college.

Scott hired the girls all in hopes that they would do well and things would go right.

All the girls seemed to get along well. They talked about their boyfriends and their likes and dislikes about food, what they did to have fun, and what they did to stay in shape.

Everything went along smoothly the first day as far as Scott was concerned.

The girls all looked like stars and they enjoyed what they did.

Scott was very happy and he was satisfied for now and he hoped nothing else happened.

"Let's all get together on Saturday and go shopping," Jennifer suggested.

"Yeah, we're game on that," her friends all said.

"What time are we going to get together and where do you all want to meet?" Tiffany asked.

"Let's get together around ten in the morning," Star said, and the other girls agreed.

"I'll drive," Samantha said. "I'll pick everyone up."

The week flew by rather quickly and the girls put all their effort into practicing for the fashion show they were to have the following week.

They walked up and down the aisle so many times and changed outfits so many times they were ready for the weekend to come.

"Well, I'll see you tomorrow," the girls all told one another as they left the agency.

When Tiffany got home, she had an answer on her answering machine from her mom.

Hi, Tiffany, how is everything going with you? Call when you get a chance."

At that, Tiffany called her mom. Hello, mom, I'm just returning your phone call." "How are you and dad doing?"

"We're doing well, and we're planning on going to Florida for a couple weeks."

"Oh, I'm happy for you, Mom, all my friends and I are going shopping tomorrow."

"Oh well, have a good time," Tracy told her daughter.

"Is there anything new with Rachel or Nick?" Tiffany asked.

"Luke asked Rachel to marry him and she accepted. They're getting married in July this coming year, and Nick has a new girlfriend. Her name is Paula Brown."

Saturday morning came and Tiffany was up. She got her shower and she decided to wear a pair of her favorite jeans, and she picked out a pair of her favorite sandals as she wanted the most comfortable shoes she could find. She wore her hair up in a bun and very little makeup as she usually did on her days off, and she was still one of the most attractive girls anyone ever saw. Star, Jennifer, and Samantha dressed comfortably and casual also. They wore jeans and T-shirts and sandals as well.

All four girls had a wonderful time. They shopped at several boutiques along the boulevard, several outlet stores, and many shoe stores as well.

Tiffany bought two new sundresses, two new pairs of earrings, a new handbag that was Italian leather, and a new pair of designer jeans. She also purchased a pair of shoes to match her handbag. Then she bought a new cashmere cardigan in a cream color. She picked out a color to go with everything.

Jennifer bought a new handbag as well; it was leather and it had all different kinds of flowers on it. It was very unique. She also purchased two pairs of blue jeans and two new summer tops as she was planning on going away over the upcoming holiday. Then she bought a new pair of high top boots that she had absolutely fallen in love with.

Samantha purchased a pair of blue jeans and two new tops and a pair of shoes and a new navy blue leather jacket she had absolutely fallen in love with. She also bought a new handbag in blue Italian leather with pretty flowers on it.

Star purchased a very expensive pink Italian leather handbag with flowers on it, and a very expensive black distressed leather jacket, and a white enamel watch with pink and blue flowers on it, and two sundresses, and two shirts, and some new designer jeans, and a pair of sandals.

The girls shopped, talked, laughed, told jokes, and had a wonderful time together.

"Let's go to the Italian restaurant on the corner," Star suggested.

"Yeah, that sounds like a good idea," the other girls agreed.

Once seated, the girls ordered iced tea and pepperoni pizza and they each had a salad.

The girls talked about everything from their boyfriends to what they did in life.

That night as the girls left the restaurant they were relaxed, happy, and laid back.

"We'll have to get together again real soon," Tiffany suggested.

"How about two weeks from today?" Star replied.

That night the girls said their goodbyes and went their separate ways and Sunday was a relaxing one, but Sundays were never long enough and it flew by in a heartbeat.

Chapter 5

Just like clockwork, the alarm was ringing and Monday morning was here already.

Tiffany awoke and turned off the alarm with a sleepy yawn. She wished she could stay in bed a little while longer but she had a routine of work to be done, as usual. She got her shower first off and dressed, and on her way out the door, she grabbed her purse. She completely skipped breakfast as she figured on stopping at McDonald's on her way to work.

She arrived at the agency at her usual time, and as she walked through the door, she was greeted by her coworkers and Scott.

She changed into what she was to wear and she was on the runway within half an hour.

All the girls walked up and down the runway with style and dignity as they always did.

The day moved along quickly and it was lunchtime before the girls knew it.

"How about going to the little sandwich shop after work?" the girls discussed at their lunch break.

The girls all ate light at lunchtime, as they ate salads and fruit.

As the day progressed, everything appeared to be going as planned when Carrie was walking down the aisle and she said, "I feel faint," and she collapsed as she said it.

"Oh no," the other girls exclaimed, "what made her do that?" and Scott called 911 immediately.

When the ambulance arrived at the agency, the paramedics picked Carrie up and put her on the stretcher. "She's stable," they told each other as they loaded her into the ambulance and started an IV.

Once they had her at the hospital, they ran a battery of tests. They took her blood pressure, pulse, and did some blood work and they asked her to give a urine specimen, after which the kind doctor revealed the fact that she was about four weeks pregnant.

Carrie was in the hospital for a couple days, and when the doctor sent her home, he told her she would have to watch and make sure she ate better as her blood sugar level was extremely low.

"Don't work at the agency for a week and don't work yourself to death as you need to take care of yourself at this time in your life, with a baby on the way," Dr. Baker told her.

"I'll see you in two weeks just to recheck your blood sugar," the doctor said.

Carrie was glad the week was over and she was happy to be going back to work. She was both happy and had mixed emotions over discovering that she was expecting again. She was happy in the fact that she would be a mother for the second time in her life, and she was kind of unsure about Eric as he was always out with the guys and he was drunk half the time. He just didn't seem to want a real marriage even with one son, Mark, and a child on the way.

Carrie knew her life of work was completely out of the question in a few short months, and she was unsure which way to turn to fill in her time when she was with child and her figure would be ruined. She would only be able to work till she got a little bit bigger and then she would have to try and fill in her days looking forward to taking care of her children.

Carrie was wishing that Eric would stay at home more and help her more with her son and family matters, but it seemed like he was out getting drunk more and more these days.

Tiffany went to see her two friends Carrie and Mary Anne quite often, and as it turned out, Mary Anne would never be able to work at the agency again. Dr. Donaldson informed her that her spine was severed in many places, confining her in her wheelchair for the rest of her life.

Tiffany felt terrible about Mary Anne's situation.

May Anne was going to be placed in an assisted living facility first for several months and then she was going to be moved to a rehab facility. She was looking at life positively and that's probably why she lived.

She was moved into a rehabilitation facility and was there probably for a long time, or at least till someone would accept her as their wife and would want her enough that they would want her and marry her for who she was.

Mary Anne was still a very pretty girl, and when you looked at her, you didn't look at the wheelchair, but you looked at the person she was. She was a very lucky girl to have survived such a terrible accident.

Once at the rehab there were some people Mary Ann became good friends with. She met one guy who introduced himself as Joseph Brown. He had jet black hair and blue eyes. He was there because he had been in a terrible motorcycle accident and he was in a wheelchair and his left leg was broken.

Mary Anne and Joe seemed to have a lot in common, and every time they were together, they talked endlessly.

They talked about everything from where they came from to what they did for a living and Joe said he had a girlfriend and she was coming to visit him, and he felt very fortunate to have someone and he felt bad for Mary Anne in the condition she was in and all the older she was.

There were two girls there whose names were Erin and Carolyn, and Mary Anne and they got along really well. Erin was in a car accident and was lucky to be alive as well, and Carolyn was hit by a driver who didn't see her one night she was walking across the street in a blinding rainstorm. Carolyn had a fractured pelvis and had a slight chance of possibly walking again.

All of the people there were upbeat after considering what they had been through and may not have made it otherwise.

After being there at the rehab for several months, a few new people had come in and among them were two guys and another girl.

The one guy whose name was Tie introduced himself to Mary Anne and they seemed to hit it off. They talked endlessly and went to the exercise station together and ate out a time or two with others and then Tie asked Mary Anne out to dinner and a movie. Mary Anne said she would absolutely love to go.

She was attracted to Tie. He was very handsome. He had blond hair and hazel eyes. He seemed to like her very much as well.

The two of them went out to see a very funny movie. It was called Night Train and they laughed and had a wonderful time and then they went out for pizzas and they each had some drinks.

"I had fun tonight," Mary Anne told Tie.

"That's good," Tie told Mary Anne.

"People need to have fun as life is short and it goes by quickly." is short and it goes by quickly.

"What happened to you?" Tie asked her.

"I was in a very bad car wreck, I had too much to drink and I got carried away and was speeding a little too fast and it just happened so fast. I never would have drank that night if I had it to do over."

"I guess we learn from our mistakes," Tie said, "but sometimes our mistakes almost take our lives."

"Yeah, that is true and it is very hard to deal with him in any case. What happened to you, Tie?" asked Mary Anne.

"I was drunk and it was pouring down rain, and I was driving a little too fast for conditions and I came to a really sharp bend in the road and I hit a tree head-on and messed up my spinal column and broke my tailbone. My doctor told me if I walk again I'll be very fortunate."

"That's too bad for you," Mary Anne said.

"Something got us here where we are today," and they both said that at the same time and meant it.

They had such a good time neither of them wanted the night to end.

"It's too bad that good times don't last long enough," they both said and agreed fully.

Things were moving right along at the agency and the girls were preparing for an upcoming fashion show.

Tiffany's parents were going to Paris for a week. They were leaving the following weekend and Tracy was telling Tiffany how she was going to shop at some of the places she was going to go while she and her husband were there.

"I wish I were going with the two of you," Tiffany told her mother.

"Yeah, I would take you kids along with us if I could."

"This will be the second time we've been there, and I absolutely love the setting there as it truly is romantic."

"Well, I sort of envy you for being able to travel so much, Mom. It seems like Dad and you are always going somewhere."

Yeah, anymore we do go a lot and we are care free as we no longer have little ones who keep us from enjoying things. We might as well travel some now longer have little ones who keep us from enjoying things. We =might as well travel some now as we might not be able to go all the time when we get older."

"I'll be here working at the agency as usual, Mom, doing the same old stuff. I'm glad it's something that I enjoy a lot and I don't mind doing," Tiffany said.

"Yeah, I'm glad that you kids are all doing pretty good."

"I hope you have a very enjoyable time and I'll be thinking about you and Dad while you are there."

Back at the agency, all the girls put in a very hectic day and they were looking forward to the weekend.

Friday was scheduled to have a big fashion show at the agency and although the girls all looked amazing they were dead tired at the end of the day.

"Everything looks good," Scott told the girls. "Try to be your very best tomorrow." There is a lot of money that goes into a fashion show and Scott had number one girls working for him. He planned on making some money from the upcoming fashion show. He also knew that various raises were in order. Tiffany was due for a raise as she had been there at the agency for about five years, and Scott was going to give the other girls a raise as well. He felt that they were worth it and he had made some money and he wanted to be fair to his employees.

The day of the fashion show the girls were at the agency early. Everything was going as good as could be expected.

All the girls did the best they could do and they looked fantastic.

Scott was pleased by what he was and knew it would bring in some extra funds. He thought that you couldn't ask for more even if you wanted to. He had other places of business reply about what they saw as well. Calls and excellent remarks of all kinds were coming in and it made it all worth the while.

"Have a very good weekend," Scott told the girls as they left the agency.

"Same to you, Scott," the girls all replied in unison.

Tiffany and her friends decided they would go to see a movie the following Saturday and out to get pizza afterwards. "That sounds like a good idea," the girls all said.

When Tiffany got home, she had a message on her answering machine from a guy named Paul Johnson. "Hi, this is Paul. I saw you in the fashion show and I'm wanting you to call me sometime soon. My cell phone number is 814-715-9283, I'll be waiting to hear from you."

Tiffany called Paul after receiving his message. Hi, Paul, this is Tiffany. I'm returning your phone call. I would love to go out with you."

"I guess this is kind of like a blind date," Paul said.

"Yeah, I guess it is," Tiffany answered.

"There is a concert next weekend in the arena here in twon," Paul said.

"That would make a good first date," Tiffany told him.

"So you would love to go?" Paul asked.

"Yeah, what time do you want to go?"

"I'll pick you up around four o'clock. The concert starts at seven o'clock. Where do you live exactly?" Paul asked.

Tiffany explained it to Paul. It's a date then, they agreed.

The girls all got together on Saturday and went to see a very good movie and then they went out for pizza.

"I have a date with a guy named Paul next weekend," Tiffany told her friends.

"That's exciting," her friends said. "How did you meet him?"

He called and left a message on my answering machine. He said that he saw the fashion show. We're going to see a concert.

"We hope you have a wonderful time," the girls told her.

The girls had a very good time shopping. They all did the same damage as they usually did when they got together. They shopped at many stores and went to lunch at a nearby sandwich place near the mall.

"The time really flies when you have days off," Tiffany told her friends.

"Ain't that the truth," the other girls answered.

The whole week went by quickly and it was Saturday night. Tiffany talked to Paul several times that week, and when he arrived at her place, she was waiting for him. Tiffany was wearing a casual denim dress and a pair of sandals and she had her hair in several braids and that was different for her. She looked like a teenager to Paul, and he was very good looking as far as she was concerned. He had jet black hair and a very athletic body. You could see easily that he worked out. He was taller than Tiffany and that made her feel much more at ease. He already knew what she looked like, but he told her she was even better looking in person. That made Tiffany feel at home with Paul. They seemed to hit it off and they got along really well together. They talked about their lives and what their interests were.

The concert seemed to be a hit and something the two of them enjoyed. They had hot dogs and French fries and popcorn, and after the concert was over, they went out for pizza and beer.

"I've enjoyed the night we've shared together," they both agreed.

When Paul dropped Tiffany off, he kissed her and asked her if she would like to go to a ball game on Sunday. "Yes, I would love to go with you," she answered.

"Then it's another date, and it's official," Paul said.

Tiffany had such a good time she hated the night to end. Paul felt the same way and told her so.

Sunday turned out to be a gorgeous day and Tiffany was wearing a yellow flowered sundress and flat shoes. She looked so young and elegant Paul was thinking to himself, and he remarked to her as well. He made her feel like a teenager. The night turned out to be a hit, and when they got to the small Mexican restaurant, the two of them picked out chicken enchiladas. They talked endlessly.

Paul had beer and Tiffany had mixed drinks. They were both feeling pretty good when they got back to Tiffany's house.

As they were sitting on the couch, Paul kissed Tiffany and she kissed him and he started to undress her and he took her sundress off and she undressed him and they were sitting naked on the sofa and then she led him to her bedroom, and they made love. Then they fell asleep as he held her after which they made love again. They showered together and he made love to her again in the shower. "It feels wonderful to be with you," Paul told her. When he dropped her off at the end of the day, they decided to have dinner on Friday night.

"Do you want to have the fish special? They make excellent fish and fries."

"Yeah, that sounds very good to me," Tiffany told him.

Friday night was right around the corner and the girls and Tiffany were all talking about Tiffany's date. "Paul is a good person. He makes my life exciting. He's always planning things for us to do together."

"Sounds like you two were made for each other."

The week went by rather quickly and Friday night was near.

Tiffany had on jeans and a red T-shirt and sandals. She always looked spectacular to Paul.

"Do you want to go to some of the shops?" Paul asked. "We have time, and I know how much women love to shop."

"Yeah, I would love that," Tiffany said.

While there they went through several stores and boutiques and Tiffany bought two maxi dresses and a maxi skirt and a sweater to go with the skirt. She also bought two pair of shoes. She finally picked out a handbag which she absolutely loved. "I did some damage, as I usually do, but I could have done a lot more if I would have had the time." "Maybe it was a good thing that we didn't have a lot of extra time," Paul said jokingly. "Yeah, that's easy for you to say," Tiffany teased.

After went shopping, they went to the restaurant for fish and fries. "The fish is very good here," Tiffany told Paul. "Yeah, they do have good fish and fries."

The two of them had lite beer and fish and fries and hush puppies, and then they had dessert.

They went back to Tiffany's house afterwards and once there they went to bed and they undressed each other and they made love over and over until they fell asleep, and when they woke up, they made love again. Then they watched a movie.

"My time goes by quickly when I'm with you," Tiffany said.

"Yes, I feel that way as well, when I'm with you," Paul told her.

"Do you want to go to the beach in a week or two?" Paul asked her.

"Yeah, I'm game for that. You're full of ideas and new things to do," Tiffany exclaimed. "With you I'll never have a dull moment."

"That is a good thing," Paul told her. "That means that I don't bore you to death." She laughed at his comment. The two of them got along perfectly together. "I'm so glad you saw me on television and called me. Things do happen for a reason." They both agreed with the statement. They already felt like they had known one another for a long time.

"On Sunday what do you say we go to the cinema and to see a movie?"

"Sounds good to me. We can see a movie and then we can go out to eat somewhere if you'd like."

"You pick out such fun and interesting things to do."

"Well, my dear, you are an extremely interesting person to be with."

"I'm happy you feel this way. I'm happy when you're happy," Paul said. "Sometimes women in your business are hard to please."

At that Tiffany wondered what his statement meant, if he'd been out with other women or if it was just a comment.

What she didn't know was that he was previously married to a movie star and that they had two little boys ages one and two. He hadn't told her a lot about himself. He only tried to keep her entertained and keep her wanting him more and more. He didn't really want her to find out about his ex-wife Samantha. He felt like a snake in the grass, so to speak. He thought that maybe he should have told her the truth and that if he would have that he might have felt better about the whole situation. It's best to be honest in the long run, he thought to himself, so why wasn't he being honest? Maybe because he sensed that she would run the other way. With all that being said, he still kept it to himself.

Chapter 6

The next couple of weeks went by very rapidly and Paul and Tiffany were planning their trip to the beach. "We'll go for two weeks," Paul told her. So Tiffany packed several swimsuits and shorts and T-shirts, sandals, jeans, and tops, and a jacket in case of colder weather. She thought to herself that a girl couldn't pack too much stuff and Paul said as well when he saw her suitcases. "We're only going for two weeks," he teased. She also packed a suitcase with some sundresses and slack sets in it.

Paul always planned different things to do in many ways that kept his mind off his ex-wife and he didn't mention anything about her to Tiffany this way. He knew this was best this way as far as he was concerned, and besides he thought to himself, how will Tiffany find out about Samantha and I unless she hears something through the grapevines.

He found out how wrong he was one day when she drove by Tiffany's house. Samantha saw his car one day pulling into Tiffany's house and she called him on his cellphone. "Hello," she said. "This is Samantha. I happened to see your car. That's Tiffany Long's house I saw you pulling into, isn't it?" She called him at a very bad time.

"Yes, hello. I can't talk right now, as I'm busy."

"Busy doing what?" she asked.

"Who was that?" Tiffany asked him.

"Oh, just a friend of mine," he answered. Damn it, he thought. She caught me. Now what is going to happen? Boy are things really screwed up now. Tiffany is going to find out about this and I'm going to pay for it.

He was thinking to himself that he could just be honest and explain everything to Tiffany, but he knew everything would end between them when he did. What a mix-up and it was all his fault.

The shit's gonna fly when Tiffany finds out, he thought to himself. How could he have done this to her?

"Well, sweetheart, are you ready to join me on the beach?"

"I sure am," Tiffany said, not knowing anything about Samantha yet.

"I have a feeling that there is something you're not telling me," Tiffany told him. Maybe she read his mind or maybe it was intuition.

"What gave you that notion?" he asked her trying to cover up his true feelings.

"Just the way you started acting. You became quiet all of a sudden and you're usually very outspoken. The phone call had me thinking this way."

"Well the phone call was just a friend of mine," he said rather quickly.

"That's nice to know but I somehow am not sure if I believe you." She was suddenly suspicious of him and he wasn't sure he liked the sounds of it. *I think she is getting wise to my actions*, Paul was thinking to himself.

"Let's just focus on going to the beach and having a wonderful time, and how much fun the two of us have when we are together," Paul told her.

Tiffany was wondering why he had changed the subject so quickly, and she also thought that she was probably overreacting.

"I really do want to have a good time at the beach," Paul told her.

"Yeah, let's forget about everything for now, and have the time of our life," Tiffany said. "Yeah, I'm ready. I packed everything but the kitchen sink."

"Yeah, I can see that," Paul said jokingly.

"You're so much fun to be with, and I'm really falling in love with you," Tiffany said and meant it. She had all but forgotten their previous conversation.

"You keep looking so attractive and I'm going to take you to bed with me," Paul said.

"We'll never leave then, if that is the case," Tiffany laughed.

"Let's go now before we do end up in bed."

They had a wonderful trip, and when they go there, Tiffany changed into a red-and-white polka-dot bikini and Paul put on a pair of swimming trunks.

They played volleyball and badminton and tossed the football back and forth. Afterwards they rented a boat and went out into the ocean. They had an amazing time together.

At the end of the day they went to a nearby restaurant and ordered an appetizer to start with and drinks. They ordered a blooming onion for an appetizer and diet Coke to drink, and Tiffany ordered a turkey dinner which came with mashed potatoes and a vegetable, and a roll and butter. Paul ordered a roast beef dinner. He had a baked potato, a vegetable, and a roll with butter. Afterwards they ordered coconut cream pie for dessert.

The day really flew by, they told one another. Yeah, the time flies when you're having fun.

"Let's go for a walk on the beach," Paul suggested.

It was such a pleasant evening and the weather was perfect. The sun was setting and Tiffany ran out along the beach. She looked so vibrant and young and Paul went running after her and he untied her bikini and she took off his swim trunks and they made love in the water.

"I'm having such a good time," Tiffany exclaimed.

"Me too," Paul said and truly meant it.

"I'm so glad we decided on this trip and I love making love to you on the beach," he said.

"Yeah, I love making love on the beach as well," Tiffany said.

"We'll have to do this more often," she laughed.

"I think I'm really getting into this," he said.

"Me too," she said and truly meant it. The water felt good on their skin and they could hardly get enough of each other as they made love over and over again.

The two of them had so much fun they didn't want the evening to end.

"Boy, did I ever get lucky finding you, Tiffany."

"I feel the same way about you, Paul."

After they got out of the water, they dressed and walked along the beach hand in hand together.

"I know our time here is going to fly by," Tiffany said.

When they got back to their room, they ordered room service and the two of them showered together and made love in the shower.

They made love over and over again.

When they got out of the shower, Paul put his robe on and Tiffany put on one of Paul's big shirts.

"You look a lot better in that thing than I do," he said jokingly.

She laughed at what he said, and the bell rang. Room service was there.

The evening turned out to be a perfect one.

They had mixed drinks and snacks and watched TV, and afterwards they made love over and over again in the huge bed.

They finally fell sound asleep until morning. Tiffany was lying in Paul's arms when she awoke.

They made love over and over again and then they got in the shower and made love again.

Afterwards they dressed. Tiffany was wearing a sundress and sandals and Paul had on a nice shirt and a vest and jeans.

"You look absolutely amazing," he told her.

"Yeah, and you look pretty awesome yourself," she told him.

"Where would you like to go for breakfast?" he asked.

She picked out a little place up the street and they had pancakes and sausage and coffee and orange juice, and they talked endlessly.

The two of them looked so good together, just like they were meant to be.

"What's in store for us today?" she asked.

"I'm not sure yet, what would you suggest that we do?"

"I would like to go to some of the malls around here and some of the boutiques," she said.

"That sounds pretty dangerous to me," he told her.

She laughed and said, "You say such sweet things and always at the right times.

"I'm glad you feel that way. You're a very exciting person to be with and you make my life very enjoyable."

After they the couch, Paul took a drive and came to some stores and he left her shop while he quietly sat reading a good book.

He went in some stores with her as she picked out some things she liked and told the sales clerk that she might be back and asked them if they would hold them for her.

She figured she would be back if she wanted the items bad enough.

Paul liked the way she shopped and he told her so.

"You don't buy everything you come to," he said. "I like that about you."

"Well my mom taught me at a young age to shop around first and not to buy everything I see."

"You have a good mother. I suppose she also told you that money doesn't grow on trees."

"Yeah, as a matter of fact she did say that several times while I was growing up."

They shopped and then they went back to the stores she picked out and said there were some items she really liked. She picked out two sundresses and some shorts and a few shirts.

After that they went out to eat. They went to a small sandwich shop and bought hoagies. She bought a club hoagie and he got an Italian hoagie and they got cookies and Mountain Dew to drink.

They had a very excellent time together.

"What do you say we go to see a movie at the drive-in?" he asked.

"That sounds like a very good idea," she said.

He took her back and he left her shop some more. She bought two pair of shoes that she loved and a denim jacket with a lot of colorful fancy stitching on the back. She bought some earrings and a new handbag. It was an Italian hand bag with a sunset painted on it.

"That looks like a very romantic handbag," he told her. "I like the sunset on it, it's very pretty, just like you,"

"Like I've told you, you say such sweet things and you are a sweet person."

He was really falling in love with her fast.

"How could I be so lucky to have met such a wonderful woman?"

After a day of shopping, they drove to the movies and bought a pepperoni pizza and pop.

They saw a very good movie, which they both enjoyed.

After that they went back to their room and made love over and over again.

"Loving you is fun," she told him and he said the same thing to her.

When they awoke in the morning, they made love, showered, and put on their swimsuits and went out and took a swim in the pool. The water felt just right and they swam and swam and laid out on the deck together.

It was lunchtime when they finally left and went to the beach and walked up and down the coast.

"I think today is just going to be a laid-back kind of day," he said.

They got ice cream, pizza, and French fries. She said, "I'm gonna get fat if I keep eating like this."

"It would take a lot for you to get fat," he said.

"I wish I could believe you."

"Besides that I love you any size you are, and I hope I'll always be able to say this to you."

He was even considering asking her for her hand in marriage.

"I would like us to be together for the rest of our lives."

"Is that a marriage proposal?"

"Almost," he said. "I was thinking about popping the question, but I wasn't sure if this was the time."

He was so alive; everything about him was new and exciting. She would have said yes had he asked her. She was even kind of hoping he would.

They were always happy and there never seemed to be a dull moment. After the day was over, they went to a small Mexican restaurant. They each got a vegetable burrito and then they got refried ice cream that they shared together.

"I like Mexican food," she told him.

"Yeah I do too," he said. It was just one more thing that they agreed on.

Again she stated, "You are going to make me lose my modeling career if we keep eating like this."

"Men can seem to eat more and no one says as much about them."

"I don't really think that is all together true," he stated. "I don't want to get overweight and be heavy. I believe the older you get, the harder it is for you to keep the weight off," he also said.

"Let's not talk about this right now," he said and they both agreed that it wasn't a good subject while they were eating.

"These two weeks are gonna go by so rapidly he told her."

"Yeah they are going by very quickly."

The next couple of days they spent their time taking walks on the beach and swimming. The weekend flew by and the following day there was a fair in twon and Tiffany and Paul went to it. While at the fair they rode the helicopter.

"That was a lot of fun," Tiffany said.

"I'm glad you enjoyed it," Paul told her.

"Let's ride the roller coaster and some of the other rides, and then we can get something to eat," Paul suggested

"The roller coaster was a lot of fun and I enjoyed the other rides as well," Tiffany said

"They have a show that starts at seven o'clock," Paul told her. "We can get something to eat before we go to it."

"Sounds good to me, and I'm having a wonderful time as usual."

"That's good, I'm glad I do such fun things for us, and as long as you're happy, then I'm happy."

They rode about everything there was a couple of times and the show was going to start so they got hotdogs and French fries and drinks.

"Let's pick out a seat and watch the show."

The show was very good. The two of them had another wonderful day.

Their time was soon going to be over and they would be going home.

The rest of the week went by quickly, and Tiffany was packing to go home.

"You look so good to me, we could just stay another couple weeks," Paul said.

"That would be fine with me, besides my time with you goes by too quickly anyway."

On the way home, the two of them stopped to eat, and they stopped at a few different places.

"I had a wonderful time, but as always it went by too quickly."

"Yeah, I feel the same way she said and meant it.

Chapter 7

Monday morning the alarm clock was ringing as it always did. Tiffany woke up and stretched as she reached for it.

She wondered what was in store at work for her that day and that week. She decided to wear a sundress to work today, and as she arrived, she looked fabulous as she always did.

"What has been going on at work the past two weeks?" she asked as she greeted her coworkers.

"Oh, the same old stuff," they answered in reply.

"How was your trip to the beach?" her friends asked.

"We had a very good time and Paul is very good to me. We kept busy the whole time and he always does exciting things with me. I almost thought he was going to ask me for my hand in marriage."

"That does sound like you must have had a good time," Star said.

"Oh yeah, I never wanted it to end," Tiffany told her friends. "Good times never last long enough."

"Ain't that the truth," Star said.

The morning went along smoothly and it was lunch before the girls knew it.

"Let's go out for pizza after work," Star suggested and all the girls agreed.

"You all did a great job," Scott told the girls. "We're going to have a lot of highe-ups coming in to view us here on Saturday, so be at your level best, get lots of sleep and so forth," Scott said. "Have a very good night and I'll see you in the morning."

"Yeah, same to you, Scott," the girls all said as they left at the end of the day. They walked to a small restaurant across the street when they left to go home. It was a new restaurant and it had just opened recently. The girls walked in and were seated and they ordered raspberry tea and they all had grilled chicken salads. They all talked endlessly. They talked about work a little and what they were gonna do over the weekend. The waitress asked them if they wanted dessert and they all had small sundaes.

"Well, I'll see you all in the morning," they told one another at the end of the day.

When Tiffany got home, she heard her answers on her machine. "Hello, Tiffany, it's Mom. I'm just calling to see if there's anything new with you and to tell you we're flying to London next week. We're leaving on Wednesday and we're staying for two weeks."

"It's nice to hear from you, Mom. Is there anything new with Rachel and Nick?"

"Yeah, Rachel and Luke are going to Cancun."

"Oh I'm happy to hear that."

"Nick has a new girlfriend and they've been dating on and off for about a month."

"That is good to hear too," Tiffany said. And then she asked, "What's her name?"

"Ashley Greenwood, and she seems to be a very nice girl. She's an artist and a journalist."

"I'm glad he met someone he likes to be around and is happy with as well."

"They are always doing different things together."

"Sounds like Paul and I. There is never a dull moment with him."

"How has your modeling job been going?"

"About the same as it always has gone."

"Oh, I'm always happy when I hear good news from you kids."

"Well, I guess I better let you go, Mom. Have a good night and tell everyone I said Hi!"

"Yeah, I will and you have a good night as well and tell Paul I said hello!"

Tiffany got a text from Paul and it read, "Hi, baby! How is your day going? I wanted to hear from you."

Tiffany texted him back and said, "I miss you so much, honey, and I love you and I can't wait to see you again. I just talked to my mom and she said my sister Rachel and Tom are gonna get married in June. They're getting married in Cancun."

"That is very good news, I'm happy for both of them. I'm coming over on Friday night after work. I figured we can go out to dinner and to see a movie."

"Sounds great to me," Tiffany said.

Paul was at Tiffany's around six o'clock on Friday night.

"We could see that Western movie, it is supposed to be a very good movie."

"Sounds interesting to me," Tiffany exclaimed.

When Paul got to Tiffany's, she had on a pink flowered dress and she had her long hair in a braid off to the side.

"You look absolutely fabulous," Paul told her.

Paul had on jeans and a plaid shirt in blue and white, and he had on a leather vest. He looked great and Tiffany told him so.

While at the movie, they had popcorn and diet pop.

"That was a very good movie," Tiffany said and Paul agreed.

"Let's go to that little Italian pizza plaza up the street," Paul suggested.

"Yeah, I wouldn't mind going there myself," Tiffany said.

Once there Tiffany and Paul ordered salads, breadsticks, and pepperoni pizza. They ordered raspberry tea to drink.

"I had a bitch of a day at work today. Nothing went quite right and Scott was really running us girls ragged. Oh well, I guess I can put up with it though. We do get paid good money so I try not to complain. You're not going to make the kind of money I do just working anyplace."

"Yeah, that is for sure," Paul told her. "And besides that, you have a secure job to go to."

"I do get that so I guess I had better not let Scott hear me complaining."

"Yeah, I agree. You wouldn't want to lose your job."

"I'm going to get a promotion," Paul told her. "I'm getting promoted to CEO of our company."

"Oh that is wonderful, Paul. I'm very happy for you."

"Yeah I've wanted this for a long time. The CEO of our company is moving out to one of the Western states. He's moving to Wyoming and he's buying a rather large ranch out there."

"I hope this is something you want," Tiffany told him.

"Oh it is. I've wanted it for quite some time."

"Then I couldn't be happier for you."

"There is a lot of responsibility running a company," Paul told her, "But I'm sure I can do it."

"We're having a really big fashion show tomorrow and Scott wants us all to look and do our best."

"That won't be hard for you to do," Paul said and meant it.

"You say such sweet things all the time and I don't know what I'd do without you."

"That is a good sign that you feel this way already," Paul told her.

"How would you like to go on a cruise in a couple of months?"

"I'd love that very much. Where are you planning on going?"

"I'm not sure, I was thinking about going to the Bahamas."

"That sounds like a good time. I would love to go."

"Well, we'll go to the Bahamas then, you just persuaded me to go." Tiffany laughed at Paul's statement.

"You always say the right things at the right time."

"Do you think so, sweetie? Paul said.

"Yes, I do indeed. And I'm falling head over heels in love with you, Paul."

"You say such sweet sayings too and I love you more every time I see you."

"I better get you home so you can be at your best tomorrow. I don't want to disappoint your boss, Scott."

"Yeah, I do have a hectic day ahead of me."

"You're the star person there so we want you at your level best," Paul told her.

"Oh I'm not so sure about that, Paul," she laughed.

"Well I am, and in my eyes you'll always be the prettiest and the sexiest and the smartest girls ever."

"Oh I love to hear you say those kinds of things about me. It is truly a turn on for me and it makes me want you that much more."

Once back at Tiffany's house, Paul kissed her good night.

"I'll see you tomorrow night, Tiffany. I'll pick you up around six o'clock and we can go out to dinner."

"Sounds good to me, I can't wait to see you again."

"I can't wait to see you again, sweetheart, Paul said.

The next day at the agency was a very busy and hectic one. The girls all looked very good and things went as well as could be expected. Everything was going as planned and the girls were told to take a short break around ten o'clock. It was lunchtime before they knew it and they had a lunch break and the rest of the day flew by.

"Well you girls all did an excellent job and I'm pretty pleased with all of you."

The evening was here before Tiffany and Paul knew it and Tiffany was dressed in a red-and-white flowered sundress and gladiator sandals. She looked amazing as she always did and Paul told her so. She had her hair in bows of red and white to match her dress.

"I could take advantage of you right here before we even go anywhere," Paul said and meant it.

"That would be fine with me," Tiffany said laughing as she said it.

"You really light up my world and make it fun for me, Tiffany."

"Yeah and you make my life fun as well."

"It's like fireworks on the Fourth of July," Paul told her. You are such a wonderful person to be with and I love you more and more every time we're together."

"I don't know what I ever did before I met you," Tiffany said.

"Yeah and I can't remember what my life was like without you in it."

The two of them embraced and hugged and kissed each other at that.

"Fate does smile down on us throughout our lives," Paul told Tiffany.

"Yeah, it truly does at that," Tiffany fully agreed.

"Let's go out to the Sizzling Steak House for our meal tonight," Paul suggested.

"Yeah, I would like that for a change." Once there they ordered ice tea and salads and steak and potatoes.

"What do you want to do tomorrow, young lady?"

"I would like to go to the beach," she answered.

When Paul and Tiffany go to her place, Paul picked her up and carried her inside and took her into the bedroom where he undressed her and she undressed him and they made love. After that they watched TV and made love over and over again. Paul stayed the night and they made love in the morning and again in the shower.

Tiffany put on a navy blue striped bikini to go to the beach and Paul remarked, "Can I take that off of you?"

"I think I'd like that, but we'll never get to go swimming if you do."

They ran along the beach in the sand and frolicked in the water.

They had pizza and pop and ice cream while at the beach.

"This is a lot of fun," Tiffany said and Paul agreed.

They swam in the ocean. There were a lot of people there this day. It was 85° to 90° outside and Paul said, "You can't ask for a nicer day."

"I agree with you, Paul," Tiffany told him.

The two of them had a wonderful day, and after they were done swimming, they stopped at a small restaurant where they had hamburgers and French fries.

"I had another wonderful day, but as always it went by way too fast."

"Yeah, me too," Paul said and he agreed fully.

"Next weekend I want to go to some of the shops on the boulevard."

"Oh no, that sounds rather dangerous to me," Paul said jokingly.

"We could go on Saturday. I don't work that day and it would give us something different to do."

After Paul took Tiffany home, they were standing inside the door and he started to undress her and he took her back to the bedroom where they made love several times and then Paul said he hated to leave but he had to get up early the next day for work, and he knew she did as well.

"I'll see you next weekend, baby. I love you." And Paul kissed her goodbye and drove away.

Chapter 8

"We'll be on the airplane in the morning heading to the Bahamas," Paul told Tiffany.

"Yeah, where does the time go?" she remarked. "It seemed like yesterday that we were making plans to go to the Bahamas and here it is time to go already."

"Are you going to take the kitchen sink along with us too?" Paul teased. He was watching her as she was packing.

"No, actually I was gonna take everything but the kitchen sink."

"I think I believe you," Paul laughed.

"Remember that we're only going for two weeks, not six or seven months."

Tiffany packed two suitcases and a dress bag, and a cosmetic case. She packed three swimming suits and a couple of cover-ups, some T-shirts and shorts and a couple pair of jeans. She also packed several dresses and a couple of skirts and tops to go with them.

"You'll be looking sexy regardless of what you have on," Paul commented.

"Oh, do you think so?" she asked with a smile.

"Yeah, and if you keep looking so sexy right now, I'm going to have your clothes off any minute."

"I dare you," she said, and he started to undress her and she undressed him and then they were in bed making love.

"This is what I enjoy most of all when I'm with you," he told her.

"Oh and I feel the same way about you, sweetheart, she told him.

They ordered pizza and they had it delivered. "I like having home delivery so we can stay here together and we don't need to go anywhere."

"Yeah, me too," she said.

Paul left a tip when the pizza delivery guy showed up. The two of them ate pizza and drank pop and they watched a really good Western movie. They had sex and fell sound asleep in each other's arms and slept till morning. In the morning they made love and Tiffany made eggs, bacon, toast, and coffee. Then they showered together and made out in the shower.

"We better stop this or we'll miss our flight," Tiffany teased and at that they made love again and got dressed. Tiffany had on a yellow flowered sundress and sandals and her blond mane of hair hung down her back and over her shoulders. She looked young, vibrant, and so alive and very beautiful.

"I could take you to bed again," Paul said.

"Yeah, you're trying to wear me out before we even leave. I hate to see it when we get there," and at that she laughed.

He really did his best to let her know how he felt about her.

"I love everything about you, Paul, You're a terrific guy."

It was a sunny hot day and it started out to be a busy one. Paul loaded the car, and as he did, he teased her about having a whole closet of clothes and he only had one suitcase.

"I only have one suitcase compared to everything you brought."

"Yeah, and men don't need as much as women," she said in a joking manner.

"That's a good thing, otherwise we'd need another car in order to carry everything back and forth."

"Oh, I don't think it's that bad," she told him.

It took them about an hour to get to the airport. When they got there, the terminal was bustling with people coming and going. They found the flight they were on and got in line with their luggage. They kissed one another and held hands until they boarded the airplane. Once on the airplane they were seated by the stewardess and she instructed everyone before they left for the flight. They were told about safety and such and what to do just in case of an emergency.

Tiffany and Paul were sitting by a man and a woman on their left side, and on their right side was a family with three little children. The family with the children talked to them throughout the flight.

"Hi," the man said. "I'm Jack and this is my wife Amy and these are our three children."

"I'm Paul and this is my girlfriend Tiffany," and they were shaking hands while they greeted each other.

"Where are you people from?" Paul asked.

"We're from Pennsylvania."

"What part?"

"Pittsburgh," Jack said. "We travel a lot. My wife has relatives here in California."

"Yeah," the one little girl said. "I have two little cousins, one named Megan and one named Tiffany like you," She said to Tiffany.

Tiffany laughed. "You're a very pretty lady," the one little girl told her.

"Thank you, honey," Tiffany said. "You're a very cute set of girls. Are you identical twins?"

"Yeah, we are." They were dressed alike in blue chiffon dresses and white Mary Jane shoes, and they were each holding dolls. "Do you know what we named our dolls?"

"What did you name your dolls?" Tiffany asked them.

"We call them our Baby Boos. We named them that because they cry until you feed them. You have to put a bottle or a pacifier in their mouths."

"Oh that sounds pretty neat," Tiffany told them. "Do they wet their pants too?"

"Yeah they do and we have to put dry diapers on them all the time."

"That would keep you girls busy."

"We make doll clothes for them too."

"They sound like real people then," Tiffany said and she was smiling as she said it.

"What are you girls' names?" Tiffany asked the two of them.

"My name is Morgan" and "My name is Mindy," the two of them said in unison. "Our dad and mom have a little trouble telling us apart. Our dad has more trouble than our mom does."

"I can see why," Tiffany told them.

"I have a mole on my left cheek," Mindy said, and she showed Tiffany.

"At least that's a little bit to go by," Tiffany told them. "What is your little brother's name?"

"His name is Jason and he is a whole two years old."

"Boy, he is pretty old then, and how old are the two of you?"

"We're five and we will be six next month." They acted like they were all grown up as they said it. Their little brother was looking up smiling and he was holding a white stuffed tiger. He was smiling almost to the point of laughing. "You're a cutie pie," Tiffany said.

"What do you two do for a living?" Jack asked out of curiosity.

"I'm CEO at our Chevy manufacturing plant. I just go promoted to CEO a few months ago. So far I can handle it."

"Yeah, and I'm a model at an agency in San Francisco, California."

"Sounds like you both have pretty good jobs then."

"What do the two of you do?" Paul asked Jack.

"I'm an accountant," Jack told them.

Amy said, "I'm a schoolteacher and I'm a journalist as well."

"I'm a model," Tiffany told them.

"You look like a a model," the one little girl told her. "No wonder you are so pretty." "I would like to start acting as well. I just haven't pursued that aspect of my life yet."

"Oh yeah you would make a very good actress," the little girls told her. "

"Do you think so? That raises my hopes up just hearing other people say so."

"Are you two going to get married?" Morgan asked. "I heard Paul say you were his girlfriend."

"I'm not quite sure yet, we might someday," Tiffany said.

"The two of you look like you'd make a really nice couple."

The plane ride was very interesting and the stewardess was passing out drinks, crackers, and cookies and chips and she was hading out some reading material to some of the various passengers who were asking for it.

Tiffany ate a snack and she laid her head on Paul's shoulder and took about an hour's nap. When she awoke, she heard the stewardess announce that they were into about three and a half hours of the flight. "We have approximately one and a half hours in which to go yet," the stewardess said.

Paul and Tiffany talked back and forth some and just enjoyed themselves.

"We'll be touching down very soon, so get ready to land," the stewardess was saying.

After getting off the plane, Tiffany told Paul, "That was a good flight. Those people we met were interesting to talk to and those three little kids were cute. That was a real good flight and those people we met were very nice. It's people like them who make things seem to go better."

"I agree about that. Those little girls would be hard to tell apart," Paul said.

"Yeah, it would be nice to have twins but I'm not sure what it would be like to be be one," Tiffany told Paul.

"We'd better get on our cruise ship," Paul said. They waited for quite a while to board and there were a lot of people gathered around on the dock.

"It's really busy here," Tiffany told Paul. They waited for approximately an hour and they heard people around them as they waited. It was a very busy scene.

"Are we ever going to get on the ship?" Tiffany asked. "I'm not quite sure," Paul told her, "But I hope we don't have to wait much longer."

"Yeah, I agree," Tiffany replied.

Once they got on the cruise ship, they took a tour of the ship and they decided to go swimming first of all. The water was as warm as bathwater. There was a huge food bar there where they were swimming and they swam first and then they decided to get something to eat. Tiffany had pizza and pop and ice cream. Paul had a hamburger and fries and pop. "They have a lot of food on these ships," Tiffany remarked.

"Yeah, you won't go hungry. If you do, it's your own fault," Paul told her.

They swam some more and then they played the slot machines and they went out and sat on the ship sunning and talking and they went to their room where they made love and then they showered and went to dinner.

While at dinner, they met a young couple.

They introduced themselves. "I'm Paul and this is my girlfriend Tiffany."

"Hi, I'm Jason and this is my wife Carrie. It's nice to meet you," they told each other consecutively.

"We could meet and have dinner here daily while on the ship," Jason said.

"Yeah that would be a very good idea," Paul told Jason. "That way they would have someone in which to talk to."

"These ships are pretty good sized," Jason said and they all agreed.

"It's either we eat together or we just get odds and ends at the food bars," Paul said.

"No, I think having good friends here to eat with and do things with is a better idea," Carrie said and Tiffany agreed.

They all ordered what they wanted to eat. Paul ordered steak with a baked potato and salad and apple pie for dessert. Tiffany ordered a baked cod fish dinner, which came with a baked potato and salad and she ordered a small piece of cherry pie for dessert. Jason ordered a T-bone steak and a potato and pie. Carrie ordered a chicken salad. They all talked and got to know one another.

ddddddddddddddddd the two of you from?" Paul asked.

"We're from Texas," Jason told them. "My wife's family owns a rather large ranch there."

"Oh that's very interesting," Paul said.

"What part of Texas are you from?" Paul asked them.

"We're from Dallas. I'm originally from Arizona and I was very fortunate to meet Carrie."

"How did the two of you meet?" Paul and Tiffany inquired.

"Actually it's very funny, but we met on an airplane. Carrie is an airline stewardess as well as the daughter of a ranch hand."

"Oh that is really very interesting," Paul said

"Carrie has brought so much joy into my life and I don't know what I'd do without her."

"I'm a blueprint contractor," Jason told them.

"I design a lot of expensive houses and motels and such."

"Oh that is very interesting as well."

"What do you two do for a living?" Jason asked.

"I'm the CEO of a major car manufacturing plant. I just got the promotion a few months ago. I used to put the engine parts together," Paul said.

"I'm a model at an agency in San Francisco, and I would love getting into TV movies in the future," Tiffany told the couple.

"You two have interesting jobs," Carrie told them.

"Yeah, I like my job most of the time, but it can get rather trying sometimes," Tiffany told them.

Jason laughed and said, "All jobs are that way."

Paul added that "work in general is that way, but at least we all have decent jobs to go to."

"Yeah, it wounds like we're all pretty fortunate as far as our jobs are concerned," Jason told them.

The four of them all seemed to be at ease and they talked openly. When it came time to order, Carrie and Jason ordered meals and Paul and Tiffany decided to get the rather huge food bar. "You surely won't go hungry while on these cruise ships," they told each other. "Yeah, they have something for everyone and all kinds of choices," Paul said.

After they ate, Paul and Tiffany put on their swimming suits and went out and sat on the outskirts of the deck. They enjoyed the waves from the ocean.

"This is relaxing," Tiffany told Paul.

"Yeah I could just stay here on the ship, but I don't think I'd want to be on a ship like in the Navy or anything where you never get off."

"Yeah I guess it all falls back to the old saying where everyone wants what they don't have or can't have," Tiffany said.

"Will you rub suntan oil on my back?" Tiffany asked Paul.

"Yeah I will but only if you return the favor," Paul told her.

At the end of the day, they watched a very good movie on TV and they made love in the huge bed.

"I can't get enough of you, baby doll, Paul said.

They got into the Jacuzzi and made love. "This is fun, I could really get into this," Paul said.

"Yeah, same way with me," Tiffany said.

They got off the ship at several places, including the Bahamas. The days flew by and they only had a few more days left on the ship. They had dinner every night with Carrie and Jason, and they had a very good friendship established by the time they were ready to leave. The last day on the ship Carrie and Tiffany hugged each other and said they would write to one another. Paul and Jason said they would send texts and keep in touch as well. Tiffany and Carrie exchanged addresses and phone numbers and said their goodbyes.

"Maybe we'll get together sometime in the future," Tiffany told Carrie and Jason.

"Yeah, there you go. That's an idea," Carrie said.

They waved goodbye and parted their separate ways.

"Well, tomorrow we'll be back on the plane flying home," Paul said.

"Yeah, these past two weeks really flew by rapidly," Tiffany told Paul.

That night the two of them swam in the pool and they listened as the band played and performed live music. Tiffany had pizza and Paul had an Italian sub, and then they each had Mexican sundaes for dessert.

"I'm going to miss the food here for sure," Paul said.

"Yeah, but if I was around this food all the time I would weight five hundred pounds," Tiffany said. "I could go on a diet for the rest of this year and it wouldn't hurt me at all."

"Ain't that the truth," Paul said and meant it.

That night they made love in the Jacuzzi and in bed and Tiffany slept in Paul's arms till morning. They made love in the morning, had breakfast, and went to the airport. The flight home was a rather quiet one compared to their vacation so far.

"We'll have to plan another vacation very soon," Paul said.

"That would sound like a really good idea to me," Tiffany said Paul and Tiffany spent the night at her place and in the morning they made love.

"Well, tomorrow it's back to work as usual," Paul told her.

"Yeah, I guess that is right," Tiffany said. "Reality returns."

"That is almost scary," Paul said, and the two of them laughed.

"What do you want to do today?" Paul asked her in the morning.

"I would just like to spend a quiet day with you and maybe go to dinner and we could go to some of the shops along the boulevard as well," Tiffany suggested.

"Sounds like a plan to me," Paul said. "What did I do? Did I wear you out these past two weeks or something?" Paul teased.

"As a matter of fact, I believe you did," Tiffany joked.

"That is a good thing if I can do that," Paul told her. Paul took Tiffany to the boulevard shopping and then they went out for steak dinners afterwards.

"I hate to leave and go home," Paul told her.

"Yeah and I hate to let you go because reality sinks in tomorrow morning, first thing."

The two of them stood embracing in each other's arms and they kissed and said their goodbyes. Their time together the past two weeks had gone by very quickly, and it was time to face reality again. It was morning before they knew it.

Chapter 9

The next morning at the agency Scott had good news for the girls. He said he had some openings for television and he was looking to have some of them in acting careers. It was Tiffany's dream and what she had wanted for a long time.

Scott asked Tiffany and Star first, along with a few of the other girls.

"This is very exciting and you wouldn't believe it, Scott, but I just told Paul on our last vacation to the Bahamas that I would love to be in acting as well as modeling."

"Isn't that amusing," Scott said. "We have some big wheels coming in to view you girls and they are going to be picking out who they want." "I think we have a pretty good chance and I'm pretty sure they'll pick a couple of you at least," Scott told the girls.

"When are they going to do all of this?" Tiffany asked Scott.

"Probably this week, but not until about Friday. I'll let you know when they set a day and a time." Scott later learned that they were coming the following Friday so he told the girls he had chosen.

"I can't wait until next Friday," Tiffany told Star.

"Yeah, me either," Star said. "This is a wonderful opportunity."

"Yeah, you can say that again. I can't wait to tell Paul. He's going to be happy for me because I just told him this is what I wanted."

"Let's all go out and eat tonight after work," Star suggested.

"That would be a good idea," Tiffany said.

After Scott told the girls the good news, the rest of the day flew by.

"We could eat at that little sub shop up the street," Star suggested and they all agreed.

Tiffany ordered a tuna sub without onions and the other girls ordered other subs and then they ordered drinks and they had cookies for dessert.

"We're gonna do a wonderful job in the acting career, or at least I have a feeling we will," Tiffany told her friends.

"It will definitely be different than what we're doing now being in the acting business," Tiffany told her friends.

"Yeah, it will," Star and the others agreed. "I think there's more money involved as well," Star said.

"Yeah I'm not sure, but I think you are probably right about that," Tiffany said.

"Well, we'd better get home soon," and they all agreed with Star. "We have another pretty hectic day tomorrow."

Tiffany told Paul when she got home and told him her good news.

"Oh that's wonderful. I'm so happy for you, babe," he said.

"We'll have to celebrate. I'll buy a bottle of champagne," Paul told her.

"Isn't it funny how I just mentioned wanting to be in the acting business and now I have gotten asked just days after?"

"Yeah, that is pretty remarkable," Paul told her. "I'll bring the champagne over the next time we're together. I think we'll go away this weekend. I'll take you someplace, anyplace you decide you'd like to go. I think I love you more now than I have before," Paul remarked. "You better watch or I'll crawl through the phone line just to get to you."

Tiffany laughed, "Oh, sweetheart, you say such cute things and always at the right time."

"When are you going to have tryouts for acting positions?"

"Next Friday," she told him. "Scott told Star and I and a few of the others."

"Well, I'll see you this Friday night," Paul said.

The rest of the week seemed to go by rapidly and Friday night was here. Paul picked Tiffany up and she had on a red-and-white polka-dot dress. She looked absolutely ecstatic and Paul told her so the minute he saw her. "You always look like a million bucks to me, baby," he told her and she laughed at his comment. "I love everything about you and every time I see you makes me want to be with you all the time." "Same here," she said and meant it. "If we keep this up, we're not going to make it very far," Paul said.

She laughed and said, "I'm not doing anything out of the ordinary,"

"You don't have to," he said, "just seeing you makes me hungry for you."

At that the two of them got in Paul's car and went about one hundred and fifty miles and he stopped at several places and she shopped. They went on down the coast where she shopped at a few more places and they stopped and got something to eat. They had a light meal with just sandwiches and salad. By the time they got to the hotel room, it was around seven o'clock in the evening and they changed into swimming suits and got in the pool. They swam several laps. Paul watched Tiffany and told her how fantastic he thought she looked. "I feel the same way about you, Paul," she told him.

When they got inside, they ordered room service and they got into the shower and Tiffany put on one of Paul's big shirts after getting out and Paul put on a pair of shorts. Shortly afterwards the pizza they had ordered was delivered. They put on a movie they both enjoyed and ate pizza.

"The pizza is excellent here," Paul said, and Tiffany agreed.

After they finished eating pizza, Paul opened the bottle of champagne and it wasn't too long till they were making love. Paul told her, "This is to celebrate your success, baby. I think you are a truly amazing woman."

"Thank you, sweetheart, you make me feel like it, and if it wasn't for you, I wouldn't feel loved the way I do right now."

"Oh, the things we do and say, I don't know where I'd be without you," Paul told her.

"You make me the person I am today and I don't know what I'd do without you," Tiffany said.

"It's very good that we both feel the way we do."

Tiffany agreed as she ate another piece of pizza.

"You look so good to me sitting there, I think I'm going to take advantage of you again," Paul told Tiffany.

She laughed at his comment and she added, "Go ahead. I dare you."

"You make my life fun," Paul told her.

"I love it when you tease me," she said. Before they knew, it they were making out again.

It was midnight when they fell asleep in each other's arms and when they woke up in the morning they ordered breakfast in bed. They had eggs, toast, bacon, and fruit and coffee.

"I could get used to this," Tiffany told Paul.

"Yeah, I could too," Paul said.

When they finished eating, they put on their swimming suits and they went for a swim in the pool. Afterwards around noon they made love in bed and then they showered and got around to leave. Tiffany had on shorts and a tank top, and Paul was wearing jeans and a T-shirt. They took a drive up the coast and they stopped for lunch. They picked out sandwiches and French fries. Tiffany had a chicken salad sandwich and Paul had a spicy Italian sub.

The two of them chatted quietly while they ate. They always seemed happy with each other, and they always seemed to complement one another. They looked like the perfect couple to many who saw them out. Once they the couch, Paul decided to take a walk along the beach and they spotted some pontoons and decided to rent one. The two of them spent the afternoon on the ocean sailing. It was about eight o'clock in the evening when they went back to shore.

"That made a very good day," Tiffany old Paul and he agreed. Afterwards they went out to eat. "I feel like having lasagna," Tiffany said. So she ordered lasagna a roll and salad and Paul ordered manicotti and a salad and they had peach tea to drink. The two of them talked openly while at dinner, and when they were finished, Paul asked Tiffany if she'd like to see a movie and they decided that was what they wanted to do. The movie was excellent, they both agreed. When the movie was over, they stopped at the bar on their way to the motel room. Tiffany had mixed drinks and Paul drank beer. They stayed out till one o'clock in the morning and when they went to bed they made love and they slept till morning. In the morning Paul said, "The weekend flew by too quickly."

"Yeah, my time with you always does fly by," Tiffany told him.

"There is never enough time in a day, Paul.

The two of them dressed and went out for breakfast. They had breakfast sandwiches and orange juice and coffee. They drove back home and on the way they stopped at a museum and both agreed that it was interesting. They also stopped at a few boutiques along the way where Paul left Tiffany shop. She bought a couple shirts and some jeans and a new handbag and two pair of shoes.

"I have a lot of fun with you," she told Paul and he said as much of her.

They got home around nine o'clock in the evening and Tiffany told Paul how much she had enjoyed the weekend. He kissed her and told her he better not come in or he's never gonna leave

The week went by rather quickly and it was Thursday. Scott told the girls to do their best on Friday.

Friday morning Tiffany got up and showered and she picked out her pink flowered dress and her red leather shoes. She looked spectacular as she walked in and Scott told her so.

The people who were there for the acting audition looked very professional. Tiffany and Star were the only two girls they chose. The girls were looking fabulous as they did the movie shots and they were in scenes with well-known actors and actresses. Tiffany was in a movie with Arnold Swartzenegger and she was in several different shots with Nicole Kidman. It seemed more like fun than it did work. The day flew by very quickly.

Paul and Tiffany made plans to go away again over the weekend. "We'll go as far as you want to go, baby, Paul told Tiffany. "How did the acting career go yesterday?" Paul asked.

"Everything went great and Scott was impressed."

"Oh that sounds good," Paul told her.

"It was fun, after I got over being nervous and everything started going as planned."

"It does sound like it would be interesting being in the movies with well-known people."

"It gives my life a whole new meaning," Tiffany said.

"That's good. I'm happy your life is so successful and you're pleased with x you're doing for a living," Paul told her.

When Paul picked Tiffany up she had on jeans and a T-shirt and he had on jeans and a T-shirt as well.

"Let's go to the zoo," Paul said. Tiffany thought that would be a good idea as well. They spent most of the day at the zoo and then they went to the park and they sat on the park bench and Paul put his arms around her as they kissed and held each other and talked. After that it was later in the evening when they went out to eat.

"Where are you wanting to eat?" Paul asked.

Tiffany chose a pizza restaurant. At the restaurant Tiffany chose a personal pan pizza. Paul chose a spaghetti dinner with meatballs and a salad.

"I feel like a lucky man to have found you," Paul said.

"Yeah, I am lucky you found me," Tiffany told him.

After they finished eating they went to a motel. They undressed each other and got into bed and made love. Then they decided to get into the Jacuzzi where they held each other and made love again. It was midnight when they went to bed. The two of them slept until seven o'clock in the morning and they ordered room service for breakfast and after they ate they got into the Jacuzzi and made love once more. Afterwards they dressed and Paul asked Tiffany if she would like to go to the museum and she agreed that it sounded like a good idea. The museum was a wax museum and it was very interesting.

"I've never been to a wax museum before," Tiffany told Paul

"Well there is a first time for everything," Paul said.

"It was around two o'clock on Sunday afternoon when they decided to stop for ice cream sundaes. Tiffany got a butterscotch sundae and Paul got a Mexican sundae. "They give you a lot of ice cream here," Tiffany said and Paul agreed.

"We have time to go for a boat ride down the river," Paul said. The two of them rented a raft and were floating down the river for the remainder of the afternoon. After they got off the raft Paul said it was time to get home. "We have about a four-hour drive ahead of us."

"Yeah, I hate to see another weekend go by so quickly," Tiffany told Paul.

As they drove home they talked at ease and Paul left her at her doorstep where they kissed long and hard. When they said their goodbyes they knew they wanted to be together for the rest of their lives.

Chapter 10

At the agency the next day it was business as usual. Tiffany, Star, and the rest of the girls put in a long day. Tiffany was relieved to be going home finally.

When she got home she listened to her answering machine and she had several messages. One was from her mother telling her that she was invited to her house for Labor Day weekend. Her family was throwing a big party and they were inviting all the kids. Her mom told her Paul was invited as well. Then she had a message from Paul asking how her day had gone. At that she called Paul and told him she had a very busy day and she was glad it was over.

"What do you want to do this weekend?" Paul asked her.

"Oh we're invited to my parents house this weekend," she told him.

"That's good, our plans are made then. It's easy for me this weekend," Paul told her.

"I'm coming over tomorrow night," Paul said. "We can go out for dinner if you would like."

"That sounds like a good idea," Tiffany told him.

"You decide where you'd like to go before I get there," Paul told her.

"Well, I'd better go to bed so I can get up tomorrow," Tiffany said.

The following day went by quickly and Paul was there to pick Tiffany up.

"Where do you want to eat?" Paul asked.

"We could go to the Italian restaurant up the street," Tiffany said.

"Did I tell you how terrific you look?" Paul asked.

"No but I love to hear what you have to say," she laughed at his comment.

"You always look good to me," Paul commented and Tiffany smiled. "You have such a pretty smile and your eyes are the one trait you have that stands out the most about you," Paul told her.

Tiffany was wearing a navy blue dress and she had her hair cascading over her shoulders. She was wearing sandals.

"You look like an airline stewardess," Paul remarked and Tiffany smiled.

"You look very handsome and I love what you're wearing," Tiffany told Paul.

When they got to the restaurant they were seated and given menus. Tiffany decided on manicotti and Paul chose spaghetti and meatballs. They both had garlic bread and iced tea. They talked about what they did that day and what they planned to do the rest of the week. When Paul took Tiffany back to her house, he went in and they kissed and they wound up on the couch first. Paul undressed her and then they made love on the floor and she was smiling and he had her laughing. They went back to her bed where they made love two more times and Paul was smiling up at her.

"Well I guess I had better get home as we both have to go to work tomorrow," Paul said. "I'll see you this weekend," Paul told her.

"Yeah, don't forget we're going to my parents," she told him. At that they kissed and he drove away.

The week went by and it was Friday night finally. When Paul showed up at Tiffany's he was wearing jeans and a shirt and vest and cowboy boots.

"You look very nice," she told him and he told her she did as well. She had on a red sundress and red sandals and she had her long hair up in a ponytail.

"Might I suggest going to the theatre and we could go to Maria's restaurant up the street," Tiffany said.

"That sounds like a plan to me," Paul told her.

They saw an excellent movie and they had popcorn and diet pop while they were there.

"I enjoyed that movie," Tiffany told Paul and he agreed that he did as well. Afterwards they went up the street to Maria's where they ate. Tiffany ordered pizza and a margarita. Paul ordered a cheeseburger and fries and a Bud Light.

"How's the acting career going?" Paul asked Tiffany.

"Well so far it's going pretty good. We're going to do a shoot in Morocco. It's supposed to be a TV movie and we're supposed to be there for ten days," Tiffany said with much excitement in her voice.

"Would you mind very much if I were to go with you?" Paul asked.

"I actually think I'd enjoy that," Tiffany said.

"Well it's settled then," Paul remarked.

He actually wanted a vacation again and said to her that he was ready for some more time off where the two of them could be together. The two of them sat there drinking well into the night. When they got back to Tiffany's place they wound up in bed making love and they slept till morning in one another's arms. When they awoke they made love once in bed and again in the shower. They went to Tiffany's parents' home and Tiffany had on shorts and a T-shirt. Paul was wearing shorts and a T-shirt as well.

"You look wonderful as usual, Tiffany," Paul told her and she smiled when he said it.

There were a lot of people there when they got there and Tiffany hugged both of her parents. There were several of the guests with beer and mixed drinks and there were quite a few people in the pool doing laps. Tiffany and Paul changed into their swimming suits and got in the pool and started doing laps. The water was as warm as bathwater. Tiffany's parents had everything imaginable to eat. They had hamburgers and hotdogs and potato salad and baked beans, macaroni salad and deviled eggs and fruit salad and watermelon and cantaloupe and they had pretzels, potato chips, and cupcakes and a couple different kinds of pie.

"Your parents really throw big parties," Paul told Tiffany.

"Yeah, they always have," she said. "They throw a lot of pool parties and they throw a lot of parties on the other holidays as well."

"That is good that they do that. It seems to be something they enjoy as well," Paul told her.

"Yeah, they have a lot of friends where they work," Tiffany replied.

The party went on throughout the day and long into the night. Many of the guests were carrying on like they had a few too many to drink. It was one o'clock in the morning when Tiffany and Paul went back to her house. The two of them made love in bed twice before they fell asleep. When they awoke in the morning they had breakfast in bed. Tiffany made pancakes and sausage and coffee.

"I'm getting used to you spoiling me," Paul said to her and she laughed and said, "I'm not so sure I like that." They finished eating and Tiffany did the dishes. Then they made love once more.

"What would you like to do today?" Paul asked out of curiosity.

"Let's go to the beach and just swim and enjoy the day," she answered.

"Sounds all right with me," he said. So that's what the two of them decided they would do. They got in the shower at that where they made love once more and they dressed. Tiffany had on shorts and a T-shirt and Paul had on shorts and a T-shirt also. They stopped at a couple different places as they made their way up the beach.

"Do you want to rent a small boat again?" Paul asked. The two of them did that quite frequently. Paul grew up around boats and they seemed to be a big part of his life along with Tiffany and his work. The two of them were out on the ocean the biggest part of the day. When they docked they swam in the ocean and laid on the sand in the hot sun.

"This is absolutely amazing being here with you," Paul said.

"Yeah, I'm enjoying this just as much as you are," Tiffany told him as they lay on the sand on beach twoels and Tiffany was lying in Paul's arms. It was getting later and the sun had set and Paul said he hated to see the day end.

"Let's gather up our things and go find a place to eat," Paul suggested. "Where would you like to go?" he asked Tiffany.

"I feel like pizza tonight," she said. The two of them decided on pizza and salad. It was a little later when Paul dropped Tiffany off and they kissed on the doorstop and said their goodbyes. When Tiffany went to bed that night she was feeling more love than ever for Paul.

Chapter 11

The trip to Morocco was coming in a couple of days and Star and Tiffany were the only girls going from the agency.

"Paul is going with me," Tiffany told Star. Star said that Mark was going with her also.

"Have you ever been there before?" Star asked Tiffany.

"No this will be my first time. How about yours?"

"It's my first time as well," Star told her.

"This is very exciting to have such a promotion," Tiffany said and Star agreed.

Tiffany and Star were told to pack enough clothes for the whole month. Scott said they may not be in Morocco for the whole time, but he wanted them to be prepared.

"Oh no, that sounds pretty dangerous to me, for Scott to tell you girls to pack for a full month," Paul told Tiffany. It was the day of the trip and Tiffany had three suitcases and a dress bag.

"You did better than I thought you'd do at packing," Paul told her.

"Oh, so I surprised you then," Tiffany said jokingly.

"I'll have you out of your clothes in no time if you keep looking so good," Paul teased her.

The trip to Morocco was a rather lengthy one and Tiffany, Paul, Star, and Mark all sat together on the plane. Tiffany and Star talked endlessly as they were best of friends. Paul and Mark got along very well also. The four of them felt like old friends and felt as though they knew each other better at the end of the flight.

"How would everyone like to go out to dinner?" Mark asked after they got off the plane.

"Yeah, that would be a good idea," Paul said. They chose an Italian restaurant. Tiffany and Star decided to have pizza and Paul had lasagna and a salad. Mark chose spaghetti and meatballs.

While in Morocco the girls did several different scenes and they changed numerous times.

"Everything looks great," Scott told Tiffany and Star. "You look just like professionals," he told them.

Paul and Tiffany went out every night and the time there passed by quickly. "We never seem to have enough time together," Paul said and Tiffany agreed.

The four of them were on the plane flying back home before they knew it. Scott was very pleased with the girls' performance and he told them so on their first day back at the agency. "We are hoping to get lots more acting career work," Scott told Tiffany and Star.

"That sounds good," Tiffany told him.

"Yeah and there's good money in it as well. That's the best part. Not to mention it is making a very good name for the agency," Scott said.

There were several more job offers in the months to follow and most of them required traveling. There was one scheduled in Paris and one scheduled in Hawaii and a couple in New York. More calls were coming in on a daily basis.

"Plan on packing to go to the South of France this week, as we'll be leaving on Friday," Scott told Tiffany. "We're doing more acting scenes and I want you to be at your level best."

Tiffany told Paul about going to the South of France, but he said he couldn't make it on this trip. He told her he had obligations of his own to meet for his job. "I'll miss you, baby," he told her.

"Yeah, I'll miss you as much," she said as he kissed her and they said their goodbyes.

The whole acting career was going along smoothly and everything went well for the two weeks they were in the South of France. Tiffany called Paul nightly and kept him in touch about everything that happened. She took a lot of pictures as well while she was there.

"It looks like you had an interesting time while you were there," Paul said. "We'll have to plan on going there sometime as I've never been there and I'd really like to see it myself."

"Yeah I can show you some of the different areas I saw while I was there."

"Sounds good to me," Paul told her.

Tiffany talked to her sister Rachel and she was a bundle of nerves with the wedding coming up and all.

"I feel like a basket case," Rachel said. "There are so many decisions to be made."

"You've always been a basket case anyway, as is," Tiffany told her and the two sisters laughed.

"Let's go out for lunch and go shopping and maybe go out and see a good movie or something," Rachel suggested. The two sisters were always close and this would be one of the few times they would spend together alone with the wedding and all.

"Let's get together this Saturday," Tiffany decided. "I'll tell Paul so he knows, that way he won't make any plans."

Saturday morning the two sisters met at Tiffany's house. "We can go in my car," Tiffany told Rachel. The two sisters had on sundresses and sandals and they looked very much like sisters. Their hair was the only thing you would be unsure about. The two girls shopped until afternoon and then they decided on having lunch at the Breezewood Café. It was a small family owned restaurant.

"I feel like having fish," Rachel said. Tiffany said that sounded good and decided to have a fish dinner as well. The waitress seated them and gave them their menus and asked them what they would like to have and they both picked out sweet peach tea and started with salads.

"Luke is going to have a bachelor party before the wedding," Rachel told Tiffany. "It's going to be decent though, at least that's what I've been told. Paul is invited as well," Rachel told her sister.

"I'll make sure I tell him," Tiffany said.

"How's your job going?" Rachel asked Tiffany.

"Really good so far. I'm in the acting business lately and the modeling business."

"That sounds exciting," Rachel said. Mom told me a little bit about your acting career.

"How's your career going?"

"Oh pretty well, but there are times when I wish I could do something else."

"I never thought I'd hear you say that," Tiffany told her older sister.

"Sometimes I think what you're doing is much more glamorous," Rachel said.

"It falls back to people not being satisfied with what they have," Tiffany remarked. "They want something different or something their neighbor has."

"Yeah, a bigger house, or a faster care or a different job," Rachel said.

"People are never happy until they lose what they have and then they want it back," Tiffany told her sister.

"Yeah, people are funny that way," Rachel agreed.

"I just got back from the South of France," Tiffany said.

"Luke and I are going to Cancun for our honeymoon."

"That sounds like a good time," Tiffany told her.

When the girls finished eating they picked out a movie they thought that they'd both enjoy. They bought popcorn and when the movie was over they agreed that it was a god one. When Rachel got home she called Luke and when Tiffany got home she called Paul and he told her he would be over on Sunday.

"Sounds good to me, honey," Tiffany said. Sunday morning Paul came over to the house early.

"What do you want to do today?" Paul asked.

"Let's just spend a quiet day here together."

"Sounds good to me if you don't mind," Paul told her.

"I already figured that would sound good to you," she laughed.

After Paul went home that night the days that followed went by very quickly for the family, what with the wedding plans and all.

Chapter 12

Rachel was getting stressed out one day and she called Tiffany up and was complaining to her. "Maybe you should call off the whole wedding if it's bothering you that much," Tiffany said in a joking manner.

"Do you really think so?" Rachel asked. "Maybe we should have eloped," Rachel said.

"Some people do and they regret it just as much," Tiffany remarked.

Rachel picked out a white chiffon dress. It was off the shoulders and it had flowers on it and a long train. The bridesmaids had light pink dresses. Tiffany was going to be the maid of honor and Nick was going to be the best man. A couple of Rachel's friends were going to be bridesmaids. A couple of Nick's good friends were going to be groomsmen. They were inviting around two hundred guests.

"Maybe you shouldn't have invited so many people," Tiffany said.

"I'd be stressed out too if I had that many people coming."

"I can see myself in that same situation when I get married," Tiffany told her sister.

"At least talking things over with you makes this all seem possible," Rachel laughed. "The reception being held at our parents' house is a big relief as well."

"Yeah I agree with you, that helps."

Tracy and her two daughters had been involved in the wedding for several months. Rachel's parents were going to cater the food. They were hoping for nice weather that day. The following month went by rather quickly and the wedding was in a couple of days. The day of the wedding Rachel said she was a nervous wreck and she said she just wanted it to be over. Luke seemed uptight and he told his buddies he couldn't wait to tie the knot and for it to be over.

The wedding went along smoothly and the flower girl and the ring bearer were Luke's twin stepbrother and sister. They were five years old and got everyone's attention. Rachel's dad gave her away and the wedding vows were made. After the wedding the bridal party lined up and greeted the guests. It took a couple hours for the photographer to take pictures. The reception was a very interesting one with all the people. Many were swimming and most of them stayed long into the night. They had a huge amount of food with quite a variety. Along with it they had barbeque chicken, ribs, pork chops, fruit salad, baked beans, macaroni salad, potato salad, cookies, and many other orders, and punch, mixed drinks and beer, and of course a huge wedding cake which was baked by Rachel's best friend's mother.

Everything went along nicely most of the night until Paul saw his ex-wife Stephanie and their two little boys. When Paul saw her they were by the pool and she was with Rachel and Tiffany and a few of their other friends. He fell for her immediately. She was a very. There was something about her that stuck out compared to most women. He was uncertain how she would feel about him. Stephanie saw Paul and he looked at her at the same time. She felt a chill go up her back as their eyes met. She thought he was very handsome and he looked as good as the day the two of them first met. She went over everything in her mind from day one since she had known him. Everything came back to her. She still secretly loved him in the back of her mind. After all he's the father of my two boys, she thought.

"Hi," she said as she looked at him. When Tiffany went to get another mixed drink the two of them started talking. "I've missed you a bunch," Paul told her.

"Yeah, I've missed you all this time too," she told him.

"You look the same as you did the moment I met you," he told Stephanie.

"You look pretty good yourself," she said.

They talked for a while and then they walked hand in hand to Paul's vehicle. Before they knew it they were in the back seat and they were kissing.

Tiffany walked down to Paul's car and she saw the two of them. She was shocked by what she saw. She didn't know quite how to handle the situation. She walked over and knocked on the window just to show Paul she saw everything. He was completely stunned and Stephanie was shocked as well.

"I'm sorry, I didn't know anything was going on between you and Tiffany," Stephanie said to Paul.

Tiffany sat crying by the pool the rest of the night.

"Well I guess it's over between Paul and me," Tiffany sulked to her friends.

"Why, did something just happen?"

"Yeah, Paul and Stephanie were in his car kissing," Tiffany said.

"Oh, you mean you didn't know?" one of her friends said. "Stephanie and Paul used to be married and those two little boys are his."

"Boy do I ever feel stupid," she said.

"Oh you don't have to feel stupid," Carla said.

"Oh really? How am I supposed to feel? I know I've been used by Paul."

Carla hugged her friend at that. "All this will work out for the best," she said.

"Rachel gets married and I break up all on the same day."

"You will find someone else, and when you do he'll be absolutely perfect," Carla told her.

"I thought Paul was my one and only."

Rachel came over to where her sister was and asked, "What's going on over here?"

All the girls were gathered around to give Tiffany sympathy. When Rachel asked they all tried to explain what had just happened. "Oh," she said, "Paul and her had a very good relationship."

"It will all work out," Rachel told her as she tried her best to comfort her. Rachel told the girls they were going to start dancing.

Rachel danced with Luke and then she danced with her dad and several other guys, and Luke danced with several women. The wedding lasted long into the night with music and the cutting of the cake. In the morning they left for their honeymoon. They were spending three weeks in Cancun, Mexico. The wedding was very unique, to say the least. Everything went along as planned, except for what happened to Tiffany. Tiffany went home that night and cried herself to sleep.

Chapter 13

Sunday morning came and when Tiffany woke up she rolled over and looked out her window and decided to go back to bed. It was almost noon when she got up finally. She turned on her TV and she got out one of her books and she started to read. It was three o'clock when she decided to take a shower. She dressed. She had on jeans and a red flowered T-shirt. Tiffany decided to spend the rest of the afternoon shopping and then she went to a little pizzeria and she had a diet Pepsi and pizza and a salad. She was still depressed about Paul and she was in no big hurry to get home. It was ten o'clock when she got home and she turned on a good movie and she watched it until eleven o'clock and it was after eleven when she fell asleep.

It was six o'clock in the morning and the alarm was going off. It was another work day and another day that Tiffany had to be at her best. Tiffany's thoughts of Paul were still fresh in her mind. As she greeted her coworkers, they could sense there was something wrong, as she wasn't as cheerful as she usually had been.

"Is there something you need to talk about?" Star asked. "You're not acting like your usual self."

"I'm not quite sure what that is like," Tiffany said. "Anyway there is something I need to get out in the open. It's about Paul. I happened to see him and Stephanie kissing at my sister's wedding. I learned afterward that they were previously married and they have two little boys. He seemed like he loved me so much and we did everything imaginable in the short time we were together."

"You'll have other guys in your life, and someone better will want you," Star told her.

The day was a rather long, dull one for Tiffany and Scott sensed that there was something wrong. At the end of the day he asked as she was leaving if she was okay.

"Yeah, well, I mean no. Paul and I just broke up," and she was nearly crying as she said it.

"Oh, I'm sorry to hear that." He wanted to comfort her but he also thought maybe he should let well enough alone. Maybe he could ask her out sometime he was thinking to himself. After all he really did like her and she was the prettiest girl he had working for him at the agency. As a matter of fact he thought she was the prettiest girl he knew and he loved to watch her work. She had a way about herself. He loved the way she moved and she was a very confident lady. Confidence he thought made a woman very beautiful and she truly was a beautiful woman. When Scott closed up the agency that night his mind was on how sad Tiffany looked that day.

Tiffany went to a small take-out restaurant after work that night. She didn't feel like socializing and that wasn't like her at all. She didn't want to be around people at all for that matter.

When she got home she had an answer on her machine from Paul and she couldn't believe what she heard at all. He went on to say he wanted to apologize for what happened. She called him and said it's over and she didn't want any part of him anymore.

"Can't I even persuade you, sweetheart?" Paul asked.

"No, I don't believe you can, you still have feelings for your ex-wife and I'm not going to put up with you because you'll always love her just as much."

Paul knew in his heart that she just told the truth.

"I'm sorry to end our relationship this way," he said.

"Yeah, I'm sorry you let it end this way as well," she told him. "I guess I'm gonna go as I have nothing else to say," she said.

At that he thought that was unlike her to be at a loss for words and he felt sorry to end it this way. He wished he could make it up to her and they could start over, but he knew that was completely out of the question.

She was still sad and knew in her heart that there was nothing left between Paul and her. Another chapter in her life was over as far as she was concerned. She still loved the part of him that she knew and she knew in her heart that she always would. He had been a fun loving guy while she knew him and she would always remember him that way. *I guess it's time to move on and get over him,* she thought to herself. She was looking at the situation very sensibly, considering everything.

In the months to come she saw Stephanie and him out and a couple of times she saw them with their two little boys. Paul spoke to her several times but she was mature enough to realize it was over.

Chapter 14

Tiffany's time went by and the holidays were coming quickly. She tried to keep her mind on her modeling and her acting career. She called her mom one Saturday morning and her mom invited her to her house for the Thanksgiving holiday.

Tiffany said she was going to Europe and Australia and Spain for her acting career, but she also told her she would make it to her house for Thanksgiving. She added that she wouldn't miss it for the world.

"I'm glad to hear your acting and modeling careers are doing so well," she told her. "You kids are all successful," her mom said, "and you all make your dad and I proud. Rachel and Luke are spending two weeks here around Christmas and New Year's." And she added, "Rachel said she can't make it for Thanksgiving. I guess Nick and Paula will be here."

In the days to follow Tiffany traveled to Europe for two weeks and she got home just in time for Thanksgiving. Thanksgiving was festive as always and Nick announced that he had previously asked Paula for her hand in marriage.

"Oh that's wonderful," Tracy said. She liked Paula as she seemed like a nice girl. "Have the two of you decided on a day?"

"Yeah, as a matter of fact we decided on Valentine's Day this coming year," Paula said.

"That will be here before we know it," Tracy said.

"We're going to get married in my hometwon," Paula told Nick's family.

"I guess that means we'll be going to Greenville, Tennessee," Tracy said. "I'm very happy for the two of you," Tracy told them.

"You can all stay at my parents' ranch, as they have a pretty big ranch house there."

"How many acres are on your ranch?" David asked.

"We have two hundred acres," Paula told Nick's family.

"That's a pretty big ranch then," David said.

"All this being said makes a very happy Thanksgiving," Tracy remarked. "It truly gives us a lot to be thankful for."

David said grace before they ate and they passed around everything that was made and David cut the turkey. It was quite a feast and they all watched movies after the meal was over and everything was cleaned up.

"I miss Rachel and Luke," Tracy said. "They're at Luke's parents' house. Let's plan on going Christmas shopping tomorrow," Tracy suggested. "I'll ask Rachel and us women can all plan on going. After the holidays David and I are going to do some traveling."

"Where are you going?" Paula asked.

"We're going to the South of France for a couple weeks," Tracy told the girls.

"My parents usually do some traveling around this time of the year as well," Paula told Tracy. "My mom said that they haven't decided anything yet, which is very unusual for them. After Christmas I'm sure they'll decide on a couple of trips."

"Yeah, a person has to get away once in a while. It keeps life exciting," Tracy remarked.

"Yeah, I agree with you, Mom," Tiffany said.

At the end of the day the family said their goodbyes. Tiffany hugged her mom and thanked her for inviting her to Thanksgiving dinner.

"We'll all get together in the morning around ten o'clock. I'll pick you girls up at your houses," Tracy told Tiffany and Paula.

Tiffany went home and she watched a little bit of TV and she decided to go to bed. She got up around seven o'clock and she thought to herself that it was nice to be able to sleep in for a change. Her mom picked her up around ten o'clock as she said she would. Tiffany was wearing a white dress with blue flowers and sandals. Then they picked up Rachel and Paula. They drove to a couple of boutiques and the mall where they shopped and they picked out a sandwich shop and they all had drinks and sandwiches. The four women spent the rest of the day shopping. They went to a couple of shoe stores and they went to the mall where they picked out their final treasures. At the end of the day they all had three or four shopping bags of stuff they bought and they all said what a good day it was. They stopped at a pizzeria on their way home and they talked endlessly about everything that was on their minds. It had been a short day to Tiffany because she thought of the phrase, time flies when you're having fun. It was midnight when she arrived home and she turned on the TV.

She went to bed and didn't get up until nine o'clock the next day. Scott called her around two o'clock in the afternoon and asked if she could leave for Europe on Monday morning. She was out at the time and she called him back and said she would be happy to go. He knew he could pretty much depend on her.

"You'll be doing an acting job there with Halle Berry," Scott told her.

"One thing for sure is that I'm meeting lots of well-known people," she said. And then she asked, "Am I the only girl going from our company?"

"Yeah, this time you are," he answered.

She spent the rest of her Saturday at home packing and she called her mom and told her. At the end of the day she went to the sub shop and got a sub and a salad and took it home and watched a movie on TV. Sunday came and went and Monday morning she arrived at the agency with bells on.

"It's nice to see you this early in the morning," Scott told her.

She was on the plane by nine o'clock. It was kind of a dull flight as there was no one she talked to that much. When she did arrive in Europe she went out to eat and she went back to the motel and watched TV and a couple hours later she was fast asleep. The next day was a busy one and she had to be at her best. Meeting famous people was exciting and people were going to start thinking she was famous as well. She was truly starting to be in the limelight and she was enjoying very minute of it. Her two weeks in Europe were very busy ones and she had a couple of friends by the time she was ready to go home. Before she got on the plane she hugged her friends and they said their goodbyes. She was really starting to like her job as an actress. She figured she could really go far and she was well on her way.

Chapter 15

Scott was there at the agency when Tiffany arrived and he remarked when he saw her that he heard that she had done a wonderful job in Europe. "I knew I could count on you," he told her. "I knew from the start that you would be my star model and actress," he remarked. Then he surprised her by asking, "You're a free spirit, aren't you? I heard that you and Paul broke up."

"Yeah, we did a few months ago," she told Scott.

He had been attracted to her for quite some time. He was just waiting till she didn't have anyone else in her life to ask her out.

"Would you like to go out for dinner some night?" he asked in hopes hat she would like him as much as he liked her.

"Yeah, as a matter of fact I would. I would like that very much," she said, and she kind of blushed as she said it.

Scott had liked her very much. He just didn't want to mix business with pleasure. He had always heard that you shouldn't do that.

The rest of the week went very quickly and it was Friday evening. "I'll pick you up at your house," he told her and they left and went their separate ways.

It was a little over an hour when Scott arrived at Tiffany's place. She looked absolutely fabulous when she met him at the door and he told her so.

"No one looks better to me than you do, sweetheart," Scott told her.

"I've had my eyes on you as well," Tiffany told Scott.

She was wearing a navy blue polka-dot dress and sandals and she had her long blond hair in a bun. Scott had on jeans and a shirt and a vest and he looked fabulous and Tiffany told him as much.

"Where would you like to go?" Scott asked.

"We have time to catch a movie before we go to dinner."

They went to a movie and then Scott asked what she wanted to eat and Tiffany suggested pizza.

"Good," Scott said. "That's my favorite food."

"It's mine too," Tiffany said. "So that's one thing that we have in common."

The two of them were already falling head over heels for each other. They talked about a lot of different subjects. Their time went by very quickly. At the end of the day Scott took Tiffany home and the two of them kissed and embraced. Before Scott left he asked Tiffany if she wanted to go out on Saturday and she said she would absolutely love to.

"Be ready about noon and we'll spend the day together."

When Scott left Tiffany went right to bed and as she lay there she thought to herself that she was lucky to have someone in her life again. She drifted off and got up at seven the next morning. Scott was at her house at noon just as he said he'd be. "You look great as always," Scott remarked when he saw her.

"You don't look bad yourself," she told him.

Tiffany was dressed in her pink flowered dress and she had her long blond hair in a ponytail. "I like your hair up like that," Scott told her. He felt a lot of love for her and he wanted her to know it. She also felt a lot of love for him. They were quickly falling for each other.

"I'll take you shopping first," Scott told her and Tiffany said she would like that very much. She shopped for a couple hours and then they ate lunch. During lunch they talked at ease. They complimented one another nicely.

"Do you want to go to the little park on up the road?" Scott asked. Tiffany agreed that would be a good way to spend the rest of the afternoon.

While they were at the park Scott asked if she wanted to rent a boat.

"Yeah, that sounds like a good idea," she said. The two of them agreed that their time together went by too quickly. They rented a boat and the two of them sailed on the water the rest of the day. At the end of the day they ordered pizza and took it back to Tiffany's house. The two of them ate pizza and watched a good movie. Afterwards they kissed and Scott told Tiffany that he'd be over on Sunday and he left. Scott wanted her more than ever, but he didn't want to frighten her and he didn't want to move real fast, being they were on a professional level. He also wanted her to respect him, besides everything about them had been about business up until a few days ago.

It was twelve o'clock midnight when Tiffany went to bed and she fell asleep dreaming of Scott and once again she was happy knowing she had another love in her life. Tiffany woke up around seven o'clock. She had breakfast and she went out and swam some laps in her pool. Scott walked over and said, "Hi, sexy!" and she looked up and saw him.

"Come on in, the water feels good," she told Scott.

"I believe I will," he said. He went and changed into his swimming trunks. He wanted to just strip down and dive in but he didn't want to scare her, so he moved slowly. He thought to himself how great she looked. "The water does feel good," he told her.

They swam laps for several hours and when they got out of the pool they decided to go out to eat. "Where do you want to eat?" Scott asked.

"Let's go to the steak house," Tiffany said.

Once they got seated they both got T-bone steaks and baked potatoes and they ordered raspberry tea to drink. The two of them talked at ease with one another and after they finished eating Scott asked Tiffany what she would like to do. "Let's spend the rest of the afternoon at the beach," she said. The two of them walked along the beach hand in hand. Scott asked if she wanted to rent a motor boat and she agreed that it would be a good idea. They went sailing for the rest of the afternoon and it was dawn when they got back to shore.

"Let's order a pizza and take it back to your place," Scott said. The two of them ate pizza and watched a good movie and it was nine o'clock when Scott kissed Tiffany and left. Tiffany went to bed that night and as she drifted off to sleep she dreamt of Scott. Once again she had a good man in her life. She had pleasant dreams till morning.

At work the next day it was business as usual. When Tiffany walked in Scott greeted her by saying, "Hi, sexy, how are you?"

"I'm fine, how are you you, sweetheart?

"I'm better since you walked in," Scott told her. "Can you leave for Australia?" Scott asked.

"Yeah, I can. Are you going as well?" she asked.

"As a matter of fact I am," he told her. "We're going for better than a month," he said. "We're leaving in two weeks."

"Oh, I better start packing then," she told him.

Scott laughed at that and asked if she wanted to go out and eat after work.

"Yeah, I would like that very much," she told him.

They had many fashion shoots throughout the rest of the day and Scott tried to be as professional as he could with Tiffany. He tried not to let her see how he really felt and how much he really wanted her. Tiffany was tired at the end of the day, as usual, and as she got out of her professional clothes and slipped on her street clothes she thought to herself how good it felt to have on comfortable shoes and get out of her stilts. At least that's what the girls all called them.

They had learned later that week that the Australia trip was postponed.

Her job was one that many girls dreamed of but to Tiffany it was something she enjoyed most of the time along with a paycheck.

"Where do you want to eat?" Scott asked as he greeted her at the door.

"I feel like having a steak dinner tonight," she told him.

"Let's go to the Longhorn Steak House," Scott suggested.

"Yeah, that sounds good to me," Tiffany said.

They walked hand in hand to the restaurant and when they entered they were seated and given menus and asked what they wanted to drink. They each ordered sweet tea and they got breaded mushrooms for an order. They each got steak and French fries and a salad. The two of them talked about work and their upcoming trip to Australia.

On their way home they stopped at the bar and Tiffany ordered mixed drinks and Scott got beer. They only had a few as they had to work the next day. When Scott took Tiffany home he was tempted to go in the house with her but he resisted temptation once more. He was thinking to himself that he didn't know how much longer he could keep his hands off her and took her in his arms and kissed her.

She was surprised in a way but in a way she was happy that he had finally taken the initiative to let her know how he felt. After all she was quickly falling in love with him and she wanted him to know it.

"I'll see you tomorrow at work," he told her and kissed her one again. When she went inside she was smiling to herself, happy that they had gotten to first base. When Scott left Tiffany's house he was a happy man knowing he had finally left his star pupil know how he felt about her. After all, he thought to himself, he had loved her from the start, he just decided to move slowly so he wouldn't frighten her.

Tiffany went to bed knowing she had a new love in her life and Scott went to bed at his house feeling the same way. In the morning Tiffany was stuck in the traffic on her way to work. When she arrived at work she was greeted by Scott and the girls she worked with.

"Hi, gorgeous," Scott said.

"Hello, Scott," Tiffany said. "How are you this morning?"

"I'm absolutely great now that you walked in," he told her.

The day was a busy one and it was over before they knew it.

"Do you want to go out to a movie and to dinner on Friday night?" Scott asked. Tiffany said yeah, she would love to.

Tiffany left the agency that night knowing she had someone new in her life and she was happy once more. When she got home that night she listened to her answering machine and her mom said they were having dinner there on Saturday night and she and Scott were invited.

Tiffany called Page and asked her if she wanted to go out and eat that night, but Page refused telling her she had to go visit her mother and she said that her mother was taken to the hospital on that day. She didn't know all the details, but she said it didn't sound good.

"Fill me in when you find out," Tiffany told Page with a sound of concern for her best friend. Tiffany sat for a while staring at the kitchen floor with a blank expression after talking to Page. She felt bad for her friend. She didn't know what to say. She made herself a can of soup and a sandwich and she turned on the TV and watched a movie before going to bed at ten o'clock. She decided to go to bed early as she couldn't even get into the movie. The next day at work Tiffany asked Page about her mother and she told her that her mother was in a very bad accident and she was in a coma and that she might not pull through. She didn't know much more than that, but she broke down crying and Scott told her under the circumstances that she could go home. He said they would try to get by without her. He also added before she left to go ahead and take the rest of the week off.

Page left the agency and told Tiffany and the other girls that she would keep them informed as to how her mother was doing. Later that night Page learned that her mother passed away. She was sixty years old when she died. She was very young at that and Page and her family were completely besotted and broken up over her passing, it all happened very quickly. It was probably best so she didn't have to suffer long.

Page called her coworkers as she said she would and they were heartfelt for her and they tried to comfort her as much as they possibly could. Page said she was going to take a month or so off after the funeral just to get her thoughts back in order. She was told by Scott that would be fine under the unfortunate circumstances.

Page was considering going to Arizona to a ranch. Someplace where she would be alone. She told Tiffany and the other girls that she would call them quite frequently to keep in touch and to let them know how she was holding up.

"You can call us anytime," her coworkers told her. Tiffany said that she would call and keep in touch as well. Page hugged her friends and family before she left.

As Page boarded the airplane she was focused on getting away and taking some much needed time off. The trip was a quiet one for Page as she really wanted to keep to herself. She was very upset about her mother's passing and she knew she would get emotional if she brought up her memories. Page read some and she slept throughout most of the trip and when she got off the plane she was thinking about how nice it was to be in an area where no one knew who she was.

Once she got organized she called Tiffany and her other coworkers and left them know how she was doing and to let them know she had arrived in Arizona.

"That's good," Tiffany told her and she also told her how everything was going at the agency. "We miss you here," Tiffany told her.

"Yeah, I miss all of you as well, but I'm enjoying being away for a change," Page said.

At the end of the day Scott asked Tiffany out to dinner and she gladly accepted. "I would like that very much," she told him.

"Then it's a date," he said. "Where would you like to go?" he asked.

The two of them chose an Italian restaurant and they both decided to have lasagna, salad, and breadsticks and pie for dessert, and they had peach tea. They talked at ease and the two of them seemed like they had been together for a long time.

"Page called and said she made it to Arizona,"

"That's good," Scott said. "Was she in pretty good spirits?"

"She didn't sound bad. She said she had a quiet plane trip, but she also remarked that she had wanted it that way."

"I'm glad she made it to Arizona and things are going well for her," Scott told Tiffany.

When Scott took Tiffany home he left her at her door and he kissed her long and hard.

"I'm falling in love with you, sweetheart," he told her. "It's getting harder and harder to kiss you and walk away."

What he didn't know was that she felt the same way about him.

"I'll see you tomorrow morning, baby," Scott told her as he walked away and climbed into his car and drove away.

When Tiffany got to her telephone she listened to her answers. One was from her mom and one was a call from Page just giving her an update on how things were going.

Tiffany clicked on the TV and sat down and watched some television before going to bed an hour later. She slept well and it seemed like just hours later that her alarm was going off in her ear. She stretched and turned the alarm off and left out a sleepy yawn. She jumped in the shower, had a muffin and a cup of coffee, and was headed out the door within an hour and a half.

Scott greeted her as usual and much of the time at work you would never know they were an item. It was probably best this way. Again Scott thought you shouldn't mix business with pleasure. The day was a busy one as usual and at noon Tiffany and he friends sat talking to each other.

Scott approached Tiffany and asked if she wanted to go out for dinner at the end of the day and she agreed that it would be a wonderful idea. The rest of the day was interesting as they were getting prepared for a fashion show in another week.

Before they left the agency Tiffany changed into more comfortable clothes. She was wearing jeans and a T-shirt and a comfortable pair of sandals and she had her blond hair down. Her hair shown in the sunlight and it looked like a sheet of gold. Scott remarked how beautiful she looked when she was hardly aware of her looks. In fact it made her look so young and gorgeous he remarked that she looked barely over sixteen and she smiled at his comment.

"I love the things you say and do," she remarked. "A girl can get used to you; you're actually starting to grow on me."

"It's funny, but I was actually thinking the same things about you," he exclaimed.

"Where do you want to eat?" Scott asked and Tiffany suggested getting pizza and taking it back to her place. "That actually sounds like a good idea," Scott said.

"Well that's what we'll do then," Tiffany said and she laughed when she said it.

Once they were at Tiffany's place they ate pizza and watched a good movie. Scott remarked about how attractive Tiffany looked and she was lying down on the sofa, with her legs over his lap. He stated to put his hand up under her shirt and he started to undress her and she started to undress him and they made love, first on the sofa and then in bed and they lay for a while and they made love once more before Scott told Tiffany he had to get home.

"This Friday night I'll spend the whole night at your house," Scott said.

"I'm all for that idea," Tiffany told him.

Scott kissed Tiffany long and hard before he left and said he'd see her in the morning. Tiffany went to bed that night happy and satisfied that Scott was in her life, and Scott was in his bed smiling to himself and thinking what a lucky man he was.

Chapter 16

In the morning Tiffany awoke and got her breakfast and her thoughts were on the night before. She went to work and when she saw Scott she smiled and he was smiling as well.

"Hi, Tiffany, how are you, sweetheart?"

"I'm doing well but now that I'm here with you I'm doing better," she told him.

"Do you want to go out and see a movie on Friday night?" Scott asked.

"Yeah, that would be a fine idea," Tiffany said.

At the end of the day Scott and Tiffany went out to eat. They went to a little sandwich shop and had subs and afterwards they stopped at the bar and Tiffany had mixed drinks and Scott had beer. When he took her home he kissed her and told her he'd see her in the morning.

"We have a big day tomorrow, so try to be at your very best," he said and then he added, "That won't be hard for you because you always impress everyone."

Tiffany laughed at that, and she said, "I'm glad that you think so."

"Well I better leave before I'm tempted to have sex," he said, and at that he drove away.

It was finally Friday and the girls all did a wonderful job. "You never let me down, girls," Scott said. "We got a little bit of profit, just in the last few months, so I'm giving raises next month." Scott always gave substantial raises.

At the end of the day Scott and Tiffany went out to see a good movie and they ordered stromboli and cinnamon buns and took them back to Tiffany's house so they could enjoy each other's company.

"I enjoyed the other night," Tiffany said.

"Hopefully tonight will be just as good, maybe better, because I'm spending the night with you," Scott added with a smile and he pulled Tiffany closed to him and kissed her and began to undress her and she undressed him and they made love over and over until they lay spent.

They talked long into the night and made love in the morning, in bed first and then the shower. Tiffany was getting dressed and she had on a red flowered sundress and sandals and she looked so good to Scott that he remarked that he would like to have her again.

"Where would you like to go, my love?" Scott asked.

"Let's go to the ocean and spend the day sailing," Tiffany suggested.

"That sounds like a terrific idea," Scott said. On the way to the beach they stopped at the mall and Tiffany shopped. She bought a pair of shoes, a couple shirts, and a pair of jeans.

Once at the beach they rented a small boat and they sailed for the rest of the afternoon. At the end of the day they walked hand in hand along the shore.

"Let's get a motel room and spend the night," Scott said.

"That sounds like a great idea," Tiffany said.

Once at the hotel they ordered room service and Tiffany snuggled under the covers and found a good movie to watch. The food they ordered was at the room within half an hour. Scott left a tip and climbed under the covers to be near Tiffany. "I could get used to this," he told her and she agreed completely.

After they finished eating Scott began to undress her and he began to fondle her breasts and they made love over and over.

"I'm so glad that you asked me out, Scott. I've always liked you and I was wondering if you felt the same way about me."

"Oh I always have like you, but you're my star employee and I wasn't use if you were seeing anyone. I'm very glad that you weren't and I'm also very glad that I asked you out."

It was midnight when they fell asleep in each other's arms and they slept till morning when they made love again once in bed and once in the shower.

"What would you like to do today?" Scott asked. "Would you like to go to see the baseball game?"

"Yeah, I would like that," she told him.

The two of them had breakfast at a small coffee shop. "What would you like?" the waitress asked and they both chose coffee and cream-filled donuts.

"What do you want to do my love after this? Do you want to do a little shopping before the game?"

"Yeah, that sounds like a fine idea," she answered in response and he laughed and said he figured she would say that. They went to some of the boutiques where he left her shop and she picked out some various items. She bought a dress and two shirts and a pair of shoes and then she picked out an expensive handbag, which she thought she absolutely couldn't do without. She told Scott that and he laughed when she told him.

"You certainly did a lot of damage in just a short tem," Scott old her and she laughed.

"We better get to the stadium so we don't miss the game," Scott said.

"I have a lot of fun when we're together," Tiffany told him.

"That is a good thing," Scott said. "I feel the same way."

Once they arrived at the stadium the scene was a busy one with people everywhere. "Where do you want to sit?" Scott asked and Tiffany picked out a couple seats that were fairly close.

"We got pretty good seats," Tiffany said and Scott agreed. The two of them were very compatible in that they seemed to agree with one another most of the time. "I'm really enjoying my weekends since you and I have been seeing each other," Scott said.

"Yeah, I'm enjoying my weekends also," Tiffany said in reply.

The game was an interesting one and Scott and Tiffany watched while they drank beer and had hotdogs and French fries. They were both feeling good and when they left they stopped at a nearby bar and drank long into the night.

"Let's stop at the pizza place and get a little something to eat," Scott suggested.

"That sounds like a good idea, maybe that would sober us up a little," Tiffany said.

Scott laughed and said, "Maybe I can sober you up when we get back to your house."

"That would be fun," Tiffany told him.

The two of them ordered pizza and took it back to Tiffany's place. Once they go to Tiffany's they ate pizza and watched a good movie they both enjoyed. The two of them seemed to laugh at the same remarks and the same scenes. Scott began to undress Tiffany and she undressed him and they made love on the couch and then they made love in bed and they lay spent and fell asleep in each other's arms.

When they woke up on Sunday morning it was around eleven o'clock. It was later in the day as they hadn't gone to bed until after two in the morning. When Scott woke up he remarked, "It seems like the day is half over."

"It is," Tiffany said as she had just woke up seconds before him.

They made love first and then they showered and Tiffany made blueberry muffins and coffee while Scott sat quietly reading a book.

"Is the book good?" Tiffany asked.

"Yeah, actually it is. Where would you like to go this afternoon?" Scott answered in reply.

"I don't know," she answered. "You decide," she said as she placed the muffins and coffee on the table.

"Let's take a drive and go to a movie a little later this afternoon and then out to eat."

Tiffany sat eating her muffin and texting a message to her mother. She usually did this on Sunday morning as she didn't have much time through the week.

"You look so pretty sitting there I could take you to bed again," Scott said.

"We'll never go anywhere today if that happens," she said.

"That might be a good thing," Scott told her.

Tiffany's mother called at that moment and Tiffany answered, "Is there anything new with you?" she asked her daughter.

"Not much since I talked to you the last time," Tiffany told her mother. "Is there anything new with you and Dad?"

We just got back from Florida, her mom told her. I called to invite you for Thanksgiving dinner, her mom said. Scott is invited as well.

"I'll be there on Thanksgiving this year, but I'm not real sure if I'll be home for Christmas."

"Why, what's going on at Christmas?" her mom asked.

"Well, I'm scheduled to go to Europe for three weeks or better for my acting career. We're leaving just after Thanksgiving. I might be home, if I am, I'll be there."

"Rachel and Luke can't be here for Thanksgiving, but they said they'd be here for Christmas. They're going to Hawaii for a month or better."

"Scott and I are leaving after the first of the year. We're going on a cruise to Mexico for a month or better."

"Nick and Paula will be here for Thanksgiving and Christmas but I guess they're going to Paris after the first of the year. I have a feeling they're gonna get married soon, as Nick said he was going to buy a ring and he'll probably ask her while they're in Paris to marry him."

"Oh, that's exciting. I'm happy for them, Mom, Tiffany said.

"I have a feeling Rachel is expecting," her mom said. "She said something about morning sickness."

"It sounds like she could be, Mom. I'm happy for her if she is. Well, Mom, Scott is here and we have some plans for this afternoon so I better let you go."

"You have a good day and tell Scott I said hi," her mom said.

"Yeah, and tell Dad I said hi! I love you, Mom," Tiffany told her and her mom said, "I love you too."

Tiffany told Scott what her mom told her. She said about Rachel being pregnant or at least they thought she was and she said about Nick possibly asking Paula to marry him while they were in Paris.

"You're invited to my family's home for Thanksgiving," Tiffany told Scott.

"It sounds like your family is going places," Scott said.

"Yeah, we always have," Tiffany said. "Even when I was young we did a lot of traveling."

"Well you're used to it then," Scott replied.

"Yeah, pretty much so," she told Scott.

"Well, my love, are you ready to go for a ride?"

"Yeah, as a matter of fact I am," Tiffany said.

"Let's go then," Scott said. At that the two of them drove out of the driveway and took a back road and they stopped at a park along the way. They walked to the scenic lookout and Scott said, "We're a long ways up."

"Yeah, we are," Tiffany said. The two of them held hands as they walked around the rock formations.

"Let's go and pick out a good movie now," Scott suggested. "What would you like to see?" he asked.

"I don't know. How about *The Identical*," Tiffany said.

"Yeah that does sound like it would be a good movie." So the two of them picked out *The Identical* and they ordered a large container of popcorn and they each got sodas to drink.

Once they got seated to watch the movie there were several other people who came into watch the movie as well. The movie started and when it was over Scott and Tiffany agreed that it was a pretty good movie. As they were walking out of the theatre there were other people who remarked about how good it was.

"What do you want to do now?" Scott asked. It was around six o'clock in the evening so the two of them decided to eat at a restaurant. "Let's go to a Mexican restaurant," Tiffany suggested. The two of them decided to go to Cozumels and when they got there they were seated and they both chose beer and they each decided to get vegetable enchiladas. They talked at ease and when they were finished eating they decided on refried ice cream, which they shared. They each had another bottle of beer before they left.

When they got back to Tiffany's place they were both feeling pretty good and they wound up making love again and again and before Scott left he remarked, "Where does the time go? It goes so fast when you and I are together."

"Yeah, I agree," Tiffany said, "But you know the old saying, time flies when you're having fun."

"It's funny but I was thinking of the same phrase just as you said it," Scott remarked. The two of them kissed before Scott left. Tiffany was standing back inside as she was in the nude.

"I better leave or I'll be tempted to have you again," Scott told her as he looked deep into her eyes. "I'll see you in the morning, baby," he said as he was walking out the door.

Tiffany had put on a gown by then and she stood watching him and waving goodbye to him in the doorway.

Chapter 17

Thanksgiving was a little over a month away and it was a busy time at the agency. It always was around the holidays and they always seemed short of girls. Scott was putting a **Help Wanted** sign in the window and he put an ad in the paper as well.

"Hello, Tiffany!" he said with a big smile on his face as she walked in. He asked, "How are you doing, sweetheart?"

"I'm doing well this morning, but I'll be doing much better when the day is over."

"I wanted to take you out after work today but I'm swamped with work," Scott said and then he added, "Maybe we'll go away for a while before Thanksgiving."

"We could go to Vegas for a couple weeks."

"Yeah, that would be a good idea," Tiffany exclaimed.

"Plan on leaving Saturday morning," Scott said.

"I'll have to start packing then," Tiffany said and Scott laughed at that and said, "I had a feeling you'd say that."

"How did you know?" Tiffany asked with a smile when she said it.

"Maybe I read your mind or maybe I just know you that well."

"That could be a good thin I think, except for you reading my mind," she said with a look of sincerity.

He smiled when he saw the pink blush on her cheeks. She looked younger than her years. She looked like a teenager to him as she said it, and that turned him on instantly.

The rest of the day and the week flew by and it was Friday night before Tiffany knew it. "Let's go out to dinner tonight," Scott said after work was over that day. The two of them went to an Italian restaurant and Tiffany picked out lasagna and breadsticks and salad and Scott picked out the manicotti dinner with breadsticks and a salad and he had beer and Tiffany decided to get raspberry tea as she didn't want to get drunk. She didn't' want a hangover in the morning and she was afraid she would have one if she drank.

"We'll be leaving fairly early in the morning," Scott said. "My luggage is already packed in the car, ready to go."

"I still have to finish packing," she told him.

"Oh I figured that," Scott said jokingly.

"If we leave early we should be down there by evening. Plan on doing some sightseeing and maybe going a little further while we're there," Scott told her. "We might go as far as Colorado while we're going anyway."

"I wouldn't mind if we do go to Colorado," Tiffany told him.

The two of them talked over dinner about everything that was on their minds, and Tiffany texted a couple of her friends and they texted her back.

When they left the restaurant Scott was feeling pretty good and when they go to Tiffany's house Scott was all over her as soon as they go through the door.

"Scott, I think you're drunk," she said and he replied, "No, I'm just feeling really good."

"You're making me wish I would have drank some so I would be feeling good."

"Come on, baby, let's have sex," he said, and he pulled her on the bed and started to undress her. They made love once and then he wanted her again and again and it was fairly early in the night and she said she had to pack before morning. As she packed Scott watched her and she kept remarking about how good she looked. She packed dresses, jeans, and shirts, and undergarments and then in a separate suitcase she packed shoes and sandals. "You are packing enough stuff for several months," Scott joked.

"I want to be sure I have everything I need," she said.

"I'm sure you will," he said.

"I would rather have more than enough than to get there and discover there is something I need that I forgot to pack."

"I'm sure that won't happen," he said with a smile. "I'm going to take advantage of you, my love, if you keep looking so gorgeous."

"I dare you," she teased. Next thing they knew they were in bed making love again and they fell asleep and slept till morning. It was around five o'clock when the alarm rang and woke them up. Scott woke up first and Tiffany woke as soon as she heard him stiffing.

"What time is it?" she asked, stretching as she said it.

"It's five o'clock and we have time for sec," he said with a big grin.

"Sounds good to me," she said with a big smile. The two of them had sex once in bed and once in the shower.

"Let's get breakfast on our way," Scott said, and Tiffany agreed.

Tiffany was dressing and Scott was watching her and he remarked about how sexy she looked early in the morning without makeup and she was smiling as he was saying it. She had on jeans and a T-shirt and sandals and she left her hair down.

"You look very pretty with your hair down," Scott remarked. "It reminds me of the times we're in bed."

"You have a one track mind," she said, "But sometimes that's a good thing."

"Do you think so?"

"No I know so," she laughed.

"If we keep talking this way I'll have you in bed before we leave," Scott told her.

"We better leave now then," she said.

Scott packed Tiffany's clothes in the car and they were off in minutes. Scott drove until he came to a gas station where he pulled off and filled up the tank with gas.

"Let's stop at the truck stop and get breakfast," Scott said.

"That sounds like a very good idea," Tiffany remarked. Scott picked out pancakes and bacon and coffee and Tiffany picked out eggs and bacon and coffee, as well as orange juice.

The two of them talked at ease and after they got back on the road they made good time. They stopped a couple times, once to eat lunch and once to get gas and stretch their legs. They arrived in Vegas at the end of the day so they picked out a hotel room and then they got pizza and a case of beer and took them back to the room. After they got to the room Tiffany found a good movie they both enjoyed and they ate pizza and drank beer and they were both feeling the effects of the beer and they wound up making love over and over and they lay spent.

"I love you, Tiffany," Scott said. "I don't want to spend any more time without you in my life."

"Are you asking me to marry you?" Tiffany asked with a rather troubled expression.

"I believe I am," he said.

"You asking me right now is kind of puzzling me," she told him.

"Does that mean you are refusing to marry me?" he asked sounding like he was feeling confused.

"I don't know, I just don't know what to say," she said.

"You don't know what to say?" he asked, almost sounding angry.

"Look, maybe this isn't the right time for this," she said.

"The right time, you're talking about the right time. When exactly is the right time?" he asked really getting disgusted by now.

"I don't know," she said. "Maybe this was a mistake us coming here in the first place."

"Oh, so now this small vacation is a mistake. That is a big surprise for me to hear all this," he said and by now they were shouting at each other.

"I thought this was the time and place to ask this sort of question, I guess I was wrong," Scott said with a look of disgust.

"Don't you think you ought to sober up first before you spring this kind of question on me?" she asked.

"Sober up, I'm not drunk," he said.

"I have the engagement ring with me," Scott said, "And I was truly hoping you would say yes, but quite obviously I was wrong."

"Look, I'm sorry. It's just that this was bad timing," She told him. "It seemed like you were drunk and taking advantage of me, and I guess it just took me completely by surprise. Maybe we could just put all this behind us for now," she said.

"I'm sorry this was all said," he sounded calmer as he said it but he didn't sound very happy or satisfied about the rejection.

"Let's have a good time while we're here. I mean after all, that's why we're here in the first place," she said trying to calm him down.

"I'm so disappointed I could turn around and go back home now," he said and sounded sincere as he said it.

"You're just being plain downright childish about all this," she told him.

"Oh, so now I'm being childish," he said sounding angry again. "It's all about you, isn't it, Tiffany?"

"Oh, it isn't all about me," she said shouting again. "You're acting as bad as a little kid, maybe worse."

"Oh, that is real funny," he said, "And you think I'm gonna take this lying down."

The two of them finally fell asleep in separate beds that night and Scott was lying there thinking what a failure he was that she turned him down. Tiffany was in her bed thinking that it was a mistake to come here in the first place.

When they awoke in the morning they surprisingly fell in love all over again and the night before was forgotten almost completely. Scott was thinking that he could pop the question again at a later date, and he was thinking that right now he was in it to have a good time.

"Honey, I really do love you," Scott told Tiffany.

"Yeah, I love you just as much," she told him, "and I'm terribly sorry about last night. I'm sure I'm not the first woman to turn down a marriage proposal."

"I didn't ask any woman, I asked you," Scott said opening up a beer.

"You're drinking this early in the morning?" she asked.

"I really don't see what it matters," he said.

"Oh come on, Scott, I'm sorry about the way our vacation is turning out. Let's forget about all this."

"That's easy for you to say," Scott told her. He sounded angry again as he said it.

"Look we're carrying this out entirely too far," Tiffany told Scott, trying to sound apologetic.

"I truly do love you, Scott, it's just that I'm not ready for marriage."

"Oh, excuse me and I'm sorry I asked in the first place," he said sounding like it was the end of the world.

"This is getting crazy now," Tiffany said. "Can't we just forget about all this?"

"I'd like to forget it, I guess I can't deal very well with this kind of rejection," Scott said really sounding down in the dumps. After hearing the way he felt about all of this Tiffany felt badly, but she just couldn't see giving into all this. She also knew that in the long run she would be the one to get hurt if she gave in and accepted marriage when she wasn't ready. Anyway, she thought, she was only twenty-four years old and she wasn't ready for this kind of commitment.

The next couple days were very good, except Scott seemed to be avoiding her in bed. He just wasn't the same person he had been and he left her know it more or less. She was feeling badly but she stood her ground and refused to give into what she thought was just plain, downright childish behavior.

They went to the many casinos and they gambled, but unfortunately they didn't win anything. They were, however, by a young couple who exclaimed that they had won a few thousand dollars.

Scott took Tiffany shopping and she bought several items. She bought a couple dresses, a couple shirts, a pair of jeans, and a pair of shoes and she was pleased with her purchases. Scott shopped some as well. He bought a pair of cowboy boots and a new suede leather vest.

At the end of the day they ate at a steak house and when they got back to the hotel Scott put his arms around Tiffany and said, "Let's make amends. We need to put all this behind us. Besides we're wasting good time and I need you, sweetheart."

Tiffany faced him and told him how sorry she was and she agreed that she didn't want to waste good time either. It wasn't long before they wound up in bed making love and they both felt much better afterwards.

"Let's get in the hot tub," Scott said, and they made love again. "I don't want to live without you anymore, Tiffany, will you?" and at that she put her hand over his mouth. "Let's not start again," she told him.

"Are you afraid or are you just unsure or what is keeping you from saying yes?" he asked.

"I think it's a little of all of the above," she told him. "I do love you, Scott, I'm just not ready for marriage."

"Well maybe at another time and another place," he said, hoping he was right. He was thinking to himself that he would ask again soon, after all he thought she can't refuse for ever, or at least he was hoping not.

They made love in bed while they watched a movie and they made love before they fell asleep that night and Scott said he felt better when they weren't arguing and Tiffany agreed. The two of them woke up in each other's arms. It was like they were one together and Scott was wondering why she kept refusing marriage. He also knew in his heart of hearts that he wasn't waiting much longer. He didn't know why it was so important to him, it just was. He still felt defeated and rejected. He thought to himself that he would ask by Valentine's Day, if not sooner. Maybe it was his age, he thought. After all, he as turning thirty in a couple of months.

"This vacation is going nowhere. Let's enjoy the rest of it so we can say we had a good time while we were away," Scott said.

"Yeah, I agree with you," she said sounding like she meant it.

"I was kind of figuring traveling out to Colorado in the next couple days," Scott said.

"Yeah, I think that would be a good idea," Tiffany told him. "That would get your mind off of all this other stuff," she said with a hopeful expression.

Instead of making an issue Scott decided to take a different direction and not bring up his true feelings.

The two of them made love once more and then they showered and as Tiffany was dressing Scott kept watching her, remarking about how sexy he thought she looked. She put on a red sundress that she wore off her shoulders and sandals and she put her long blond hair up in a ponytail.

"You look so sensuous to me I would make love to you again, baby," Scott said when he looked deep into her eyes, and he kissed her.

"We better leave before you get any ideas and we end up in bed again."

They traveled all day, stopping several times to get gas, stretch their legs, and get something to eat and drink. It was eight o'clock when they got to Colorado and they got a motel room first and then they decided to get something to eat. "Let's get something simple like subs," Tiffany said, "since it's later in the day."

"Yeah, that sounds like a good idea," Scott added.

"I don't like to eat very much when it's this late in the night," she said.

After they ate they stopped at the bar and Scott drank beer and Tiffany had mixed drinks. They got back to the motel later in the night and they spent the rest of the night making love till they fell asleep.

In the morning they made love and they showered together and made love in the shower and as Tiffany dressed Scott remarked how beautiful he thought she was and she laughed and said, "You are such a tease."

"Oh, I'm not teasing you, I'm telling you the truth," he said in a loving voice. "You better watch or I'll have your clothes off again."

"Oh I figured you'd say that," she said.

She had on jeans and a T-shirt and a fancy pair of boots and she left her blond hair down cascading over her shoulders and down her back.

"You look absolutely fabulous," Scott said with a sly expression.

She laughed and said, "We better leave before anything else happens and we wind up in bed again."

"Do you think so?" he asked. "What makes you think that?"

"I think I know you pretty well by now, Scott."

"Oh do you know?" he laughed as he said it.

They got a continental breakfast at the hotel. They had toast, coffee, and muffins.

"Let's go site seeing today," Scott said.

The weather there was absolutely gorgeous. It was in the eighties and the two of them were having a wonderful time. It was noon when they stopped for hamburgers and fries and drinks. "I wish we could travel and see different sites like this all the time," Tiffany said and Scott agreed that would be very nice as well. "The trouble is we're both young yet and we need to work in order to keep an income to have money to enjoy ourselves this way," Scott said.

"Yeah, you would have to bring up the harsh reality of work, wouldn't you?" she said.

"As much as I hated to, yeah I did," he said.

The two of them decided to rent a raft for the afternoon and they spent the rest of the day rafting. The day was over before they knew it. "Time sure flies when you're having fun," Scott said.

"Yeah, that is a well-known saying and it is the truth," Tiffany said.

"Our vacation will be over in three days," Scott said.

"Yeah, I know," she said. "That makes me very sad."

"Let's make plans to go on a big vacation," Scott said.

"Where are we gonna go this time?" Tiffany asked.

"Where do you want to go, sweetheart?"

"Uh, I don't know," Tiffany said with a very big smile.

"I was thinking about Venice, Italy," Scott said.

"That would be a good place to go, or else the South of France would be another good place to go." Tiffany said.

"You decide, sweetie," Scott said. "We won't be going till after the New Year. You make the call," he told her.

"That's good as it gives me a couple of months to decide," she said.

"I was thinking about going around Valentine's Day," Scott said with a sly smile. He was thinking about asking her to marry him again in hopes that she would say yes this time and she asked what he was up to when she saw his smile.

"Oh, nothing. I just want to go on a decent vacation," he told her.

They decided to get a bucket of chicken and take it back to their room. They got chicken and mashed potatoes and gravy and French fries and drinks.

Once they got to the room Scott said first things first and they made love and Tiffany dressed in one of Scott's big shirts and they watched a movie while they ate.

"I hate to see our vacation end so soon," Scott said as he ate a piece of chicken.

"Yeah, me too," Tiffany agreed completely.

"I like the way you look sitting there with hardly anything on," he told her.

"Oh, do you really?" she asked.

"Yeah, I do," he exclaimed. "Maybe I'll just take you back to bed and take advantage of you again," he told her.

"Go ahead, I dare you," she said. The two of them ended up making love over and over again.

"Did anyone ever tell you that you have pretty features?" Scott asked with a smile.

Tiffany laughed and blushed mildly and answered, "I have been told that by some people."

"Your eyes tell a lot about you. I can tell how you feel when I look into your eyes, Tiffany."

"That's funny," she told him, "because I can read your eyes as well."

"I guess that's something we have in common then," Scott said, "and as I get to know you I'm finding we have a lot in common."

"Do you think so?" Tiffany asked. "

"No, I say so," he said and he was caressing her lips with his finger as he said it.

The two of them made love again and they fell asleep in each other's arms and slept till morning.

"I don't think I moved at all last night," Scott said.

"I don't think I did either," she said and they made love again at that.

They showered and made love in the shower and as they dressed Scott was watching her remarking how beautiful she was early in the morning.

"Oh stop it," she joked, "you just want more attention."

"Yeah I am. You can say that again," he teased.

They were so compatible he just couldn't see why she wouldn't agree with marriage. He tried to put that thought out of his mind as he packed his suitcase getting ready to make the trip home. They got breakfast at a fast food restaurant. "Where do you want to stop?" Scott asked.

"Let's stop at McDonald's," she said.

"Yeah, that is a popular place to stop," he said. "Better known as the golden arches," he joked.

They got coffee and egg McMuffins and Scott was watching her as she ate and he told her, "We'll be home tomorrow night. We'll stop again tonight at a motel." He was kind of quiet and she casually asked him if there was something wrong.

"No not really," he answered. "I just hate to see our vacation end so soon."

"We'll be taking another vacation real soon."

Scott still had the fact that she had refused marriage in the back of his mind and he didn't want to stir things up but he was having a very hard time containing his thoughts. He just couldn't forget about it like she thought he ought to.

"How could she do something so disgusting?" he thought.

The two of them traveled throughout the day and Scott seemed unduly quiet and she was really starting to wonder what was wrong.

Scott got a call on his cell phone around eight o'clock that night and it was devastating. It was about his dad. He was in the hospital and they were running a battery of tests on him and his mom said she would keep him informed. She said he got really delirious at work so they called the ambulance. She said she really didn't know much more than that. When he got off the phone he didn't look well.

"What was that about?" Tiffany asked with a look of concern.

"Oh, it was a call from my mom. She said my dad just about passed out at work. They're running a lot of tests on him. She said she'd keep me informed."

"That's too bad. I'm sorry, Scott."

"It's just something to depress me more," he said.

"Look, I'm sorry you're depressed," she said trying to get him to realize that not everything goes your way all the time.

"Let's go out to that little burger joint up the road," Scott suggested.

"Yeah that would be an excellent idea," she agreed. "Maybe it'll help you take your mind off things."

"Yeah, it can't hurt anything," he said, starting to sound like he was lightening up a little.

The two of them got burgers and fries and Scott drank beer and Tiffany had mixed drinks.

The two of them talked a little less than usual but when they got back to the motel Scott couldn't resist temptation and they wound up in bed making love.

Scott caressed her lips and ran his fingers through her long blond hair and the passion was so intense they lost it over and over again, making intense love. Scott even got the thought in his mind that he wanted to make her pregnant. He was thinking to himself that she wouldn't refuse marriage then.

"I love you so much, Tiffany," and "I love you as much," she said. At that he thought he wasn't sure about that statement, but he put it in the back of his mind for the time being.

The two of them watched a movie and fell asleep till morning. "I guess this vacation is over," Scott said. "I hope you had fun," he said and at that she kind of looked up with a puzzled expression.

"Look ,Tiffany, I'm sorry for the way I treated you," but he was also thinking to himself that he was gone get his way when it was all said and done.

"We need to make amends for life is very short," Scott said. She agreed with him about that statement.

The two of them showered and dressed and they were back on the road headed home within two hours. The trip home was kind of quiet and when they reached home Scott's mom called with more information about his dad. She said he appeared to be full of cancer and they were going to operate the day after Thanksgiving.

"I don't know, mom, that doesn't sound good," Scott said.

"Yeah, I agree," she said. "I don't think they'll catch all the cancer with just one operation."

"How old is your dad?" Tiffany asked with a look of concern.

"He's fifty-four and I'm afraid he's dying."

"I'm sorry about all this, Scott, I just don't know what to say."

Tiffany made chicken and baked potatoes for dinner and salad. Scott said he's spend the night and they had one more day together as tomorrow was Sunday.

"This Thursday is Thanksgiving," Scott said. "I think I'm gonna go see my dad tomorrow. Do you want to go with me?" Scott asked.

"Yeah, I think I should," she said.

Tiffany felt bad but she didn't know what to say or do.

"The chicken and potatoes are very good, baby," Scott said.

"I'm glad you like them," she said, sitting there with one of Scott's big shirts on and nothing else.

"You look mighty cute sitting there, sweetheart," he told her.

She smiled at his comment.

"I'll have you in bed before very long if you keep this up," he told her and she laughed as he said it. He picked her up and carried her into the bedroom and they made love over and over again and they talked until they fell asleep in each other's arms and slept until morning. When they awoke that morning they made love first and then Tiffany made breakfast. They showered and they decided to go out for the day. They decided on going out to dinner and a movie.

"Oh, let's go to see your dad this morning as I promised you we would," Tiffany said.

"Yeah, that's right," Scott said. So the two of them went to see his dad.

"You never told me your dad's name," Tiffany exclaimed.

"His name is Douglas," Scott told her.

When they arrived at the hospital Scott's dad didn't look good and his mom looked devastated as expected.

"I'm sorry, Mom," Scott said as he hugged her.

"This is Tiffany Long. We've been going out for a few months now," Scott said as he introduced her to his mom.

"I'm happy to meet you," his mom said as she hugged her.

"I'm happy to meet you as well, but not under these circumstances," Tiffany said.

"It came on very quickly," Carrie said. The doctor came in then to check his vitals and Scott and Tiffany stepped into the hallway.

"What's you mom's name?" Tiffany asked.

"Her name is Carrie," Scott told her.

The two of them stayed a couple hours and then Scott said to his mom that they had plans for the rest of the day.

"It was nice to meet you, Tiffany," Scott's mom said before they left. She told them to have a good day.

"It doesn't look very good," Scott said several times after they left, and Tiffany said she was sorry this was happening.

"Your mom seemed friendly," she told Scott. "I feel bad for her."

The two of them saw a movie they both enjoyed and they had popcorn and nachos and pop. "That was a good movie," Scott said as they left the theatre and Tiffany agreed as much. "Do you want to look around in any of the stores?" Scott asked.

"Yeah, let's go to a couple of the boutiques," Tiffany suggested.

She bought a couple items and Scott looked around as well. Afterwards they went out to eat at an Italian restaurant. They both chose manicotti rolls and buns and salad and mixed drinks. Scott had a piece of chocolate cake and Tiffany had ice cream for dessert. At the end of the day they went to Tiffany's and made love, and as Scott left he said he was sorry to see their time together end, and Tiffany agreed as much. As Scott went to bed that night he was thinking about his dad and his big rejection with his marriage proposal to Tiffany and he fell asleep somewhat disgusted. As Tiffany fell asleep she dreamt of Scott in hopes that all was well with him.

Chapter 18

Thanksgiving was very seasonal as usual and Tiffany's parents went all out to have a good holiday. Nick and Paula were kissing and hugging one another as they all watched a movie after the big feast. "I love you, Paula," Nick told her several times and it was like, "Why don't you two get a room?"

"I feel like a stuffed pig," Scott remarked. He felt as though he'd overeaten.

"We could probably all say that," Tiffany's dad said with a grin. "People probably put on five pounds or more over the holidays alone," Tracy said.

They all talked and laughed and got along very well and had a good time.

"I miss Rachel and Luke," Tracy said.

"Is Rachel expecting, mom?" Tiffany asked.

"Yeah, she is. She's about two months along," Tracy told the family.

"That's good news," Tiffany said. "Does she want a boy or a girl?" Tiffany asked.

"Well I don't think that it really matters to her for the first one."

They talked about a lot of different subjects and it turned out to be a very good day. Tracy thanked everyone for coming at the end of the day and it was around ten o'clock when they all left Tiffany's parent's place.

"I'll stay at your place tonight," Scott said as he opened a bottle of champagne.

"Sounds good as far as I'm concerned," she told him with a big grin.

"I think I'm getting spoiled being around you all the time," he told her, laughing as he said it.

"Yeah, I think you're right," she said and he began caressing her breasts and her lips and he pulled her so close she could hardly breathe. The two of them wound up in bed making love.

He knew in his heart that he was going to ask her again to marry him. He also knew he wasn't going to accept another letdown. He wasn't going to leave her at all. He was just going to be more persuasive. Hopefully she'll say yes the next time, he thought to himself. At that he tried to put it all in the back of his mind and focus on Tiffany.

"Well, I'm leaving for Europe the day after next," Tiffany said. "I'm all packed and ready to go."

"I'm really going to miss you badly, baby," Scott said. "I was gonna go with you but it just so happens that I'm bombarded with work here," he told her.

"That's too bad as I wanted you to go as well," she said.

"I want you to hurry back before Christmas," Scott told her.

"Yeah and I certainly want to be back before Christmas. I don't want to miss it," she said with a look that was sincere.

The night was over and it was morning already and Scott lay in bed running his fingers through Tiffany's hair. They made love and they talked endlessly and Scott remembered that his dad was having his operation today. "

"I hope the operation is successful," Tiffany told Scott.

"Yeah, so do I," he said, "but I'm sorry to say that I kind of have my doubts about it."

The two of them showered and they made love while in the shower and they dressed and on the way to the hospital they got breakfast. "We can go Christmas shopping after we leave the hospital," Scott told her.

When they got to the hospital they were told by Scott's mother that they had just wheeled his dad into the operating room.

"We just came to give you some emotional support," Scott told his mom.

"Well I'm very grateful to you two kids for coming in to see me," Carrie told them with a look of concern. Tiffany looked in her eyes and she could see a lot of Scott in them as his eyes were the same hazel color and they were shaped much the same way. It was nearly noon till they wheeled him back from the recovery room and he was able to talk and Scott introduced him to Tiffany. Scott and Tiffany stayed and talked back and forth for a while and Scott told his dad to hang in there and get better. His dad looked at him with a small smile and said, "I'm surely gonna try."

"We're gonna leave now, Mom, as we wanted to go Christmas shopping," Scott said and his mom told them to enjoy themselves and have a good time. The two of them shopped for a couple hours and then they decided to stop for lunch. The sky was a mass of clouds above and it was beginning to look like rain. Tiffany had many treasures by the day's end, and Scott had bought a few precious items for Tiffany which he knew she would love and appreciate. The two of them walked in the pouring rain to Tiffany's lace at the days end and they felt like drowned rats when they got there. Scott was going to leave her at her doorstep, but he decided he wanted her once more and she invited him in and it really didn't take much persuading and the two of them wound up in bed making love.

Before Scott left he kissed Tiffany inside the door and she was standing inside so you couldn't see her as she was in the nude. She watched him and he waved as he climbed in his car and pulled out of the driveway. He called about an hour later and told her to have a good trip to Europe, and he's really miss her and to hurry back as soon as possible. She was smiling on her end as she listened to him and she said she would miss him as much and she was going to try and hurry back. Tiffany showered and went to bed that night thinking of Scott and her next day, which she knew would be a busy one. She fell asleep peacefully listening to the thunder and lightning storm and the rain pouring on her roof.

Scott went to bed at his place listening to the rain and thinking of Tiffany and he drifted off as well and slept till morning.

Tiffany drove to the airport the next day and as she boarded the airplane she felt lonely and alone without Scott. The flight was long and quiet and she was grateful when they finally landed in Europe. Everything was pretty much planned for her once she got there and she was glad about that. What she didn't realize was what was in store for her in the days to come.

The next day after she got there they were going to do photo shoots and as she got ready she wasn't sure what to expect. She dressed in a long silky off-the-shoulder gown in red and high-heeled black velvet sandals and her hair was up in a neat bun. She had done her own makeup, which she always did. As she got into the limousine outside she was a bit nervous. Her security guards were right with her and they talked to her in order to calm her down. Getting out of the limo and making her way to the runway there were mobs of people and they all had their hands extended just to touch her dress, her hair, her skin, any part of her, just to say they had touched her. There were cameras and photographers and bright lights everywhere. One man grabbed her dress where she had the slit up to her thigh and it tore higher and tears started to sting her eyes when that happened. Greg was her one security guard and he had her black gloved hands in his as that happened and he tried to reassure her that it was all going to be all right.

"I don't know for sure," she told him, "as this has never happened before and I didn't expect all this."

"Yeah, I know," he kept saying, "just hang in here it'll get better." At one point she stepped on her dress as it had gotten under her one sandal and it kind of tore under her foot. Once she got to the makeup and dressing room she began to feel a little better as she was with others who were in her same situation. She met one girl as soon as she arrived, whose name was Hope Moor and they seemed to have a lot to talk about.

"This job isn't always fun and glamorous," Hope told Tiffany once she kind of settled down and began to rest and be a little more at ease.

"Yeah I can see that as I really got a rude awakening first thing this morning. My dress tore twice, once when a man grabbed it and once when I accidentally stepped on it."

"Sorry about all that," Hope said. "I know about how you feel as that same sort of stuff has happened to me as well."

Tiffany was on the set within a couple of hours. They touched up her makeup and she was dressed in her first outfit and ready for the cameras. What she didn't know was a little later she was going to be in a couple of nude scenes, probably in the next few days.

The day was a hectic one and Tiffany was happy when it was finally over. Once she got back to the motel she changed and she called room service and ordered pizza. Her cell phone was ringing and when she picked it up it was Scott on the other end.

"Hello, baby, how was your day?" he asked.

"Hectic." she answered. "Very hectic and unpredictable. I can't wait to get home again."

"Hopefully because you miss me and want to get back home to me," he told her as he waited for an answer.

"Yeah that and all this is more than I bargained for," she told him.

"Fill me in, sweetheart," he said. "Was it that bad?"

"It was at first when I arrived. A guy grabbed my dress and tore it and as I was walking I almost tripped over my dress. It tore under my foot. Everything started to settle down after I got there as I met a good friend. Her name is Hope. We talked quite a bit and she seems nice. I ordered pizza and I think they're outside my door as the doorbell is ringing," she told Scott.

"I'll call you back, babe," he said. "Hang in there and don't give up. You're gonna make it and be a huge success."

"I'm glad someone thinks so," she told him sounding almost at tears. She gave the pizza delivery guy a tip as she took the pizza box from him. She turned on the TV and sat down and was happy the day was finally over as she tried to relax and focus on the movie that was on. She ate her pizza and she thought about Scott and her busy day and she knew the rest of her time in Europe was going to be hectic. She was eating a piece of pizza when he called the second time and she answered this time sounding calmer and Scott was happy about that.

"Do you feel better now that you've had time to eat and relax a little?" Scott asked sounding concerned.

"Yeah, in fact I do," she said. "I feel much better now that I've had a little bit of time to myself."

"That's good to hear," Scott told her. "It sounds so good to hear your voice," he said. "I miss you so much," he said, "my day was a hectic one and very busy as well. I got a call from my mom. She said my dad is stable right now, but he is on a lot of different kinds of medicine and some pain medication as well as other medicine. He's going to be on chemotherapy if he does make it and my mom broke down crying several times while I talked to her."

"I'm so sorry to hear all of that about your dad," she told him. "It's good to hear from you too, Scott, and I miss you so much as well."

"I've got a lot of work to do here at the agency," Scott said. "I'm going to hire a couple more girls as I'm swamped right now and I can use the extra help," Scott told Tiffany. "Well I'll talk to you tomorrow night, baby," Scott told her.

"Sounds good I guess anyway," she said. "I'll talk to you tomorrow night. I love you and I'll dream about you tonight, sweetheart," she told him.

On his end he was smiling at her comment. "I'll dream about you as well," he told her.

At that they hung up and when they went to bed that night they dreamt of one another.

The next day and the rest of the week were busy ones for Tiffany and Scott. They called one another every night to give each other updates on their days and let the other partner know how they were doing. It was Friday night and they were both extremely lonely and Scott called as usual. They talked and it seemed like Scott was unusually quiet and Tiffany questioned him as to whether there was something wrong or if something was bothering him.

"No, I'm just extremely lonely and I miss you badly," he replied.

"Yeah, I miss you as much," she told him sounding sincere.

"I can hardly wait for you to come home to me," he told her. "It's gonna be a long boring weekend for me," Scott said.

"It's not gonna be much better here in Europe for me," she said. "I think I have a half a day of work tomorrow as far as I know," Tiffany told Scott.

"I can't wait till Christmas because at least you would be home here with me," he told her.

"Yeah I can't wait till Christmas either," Tiffany said.

"Well, I'll talk to you sometime tomorrow, Tiffany. Why don't you call me after work?"

"I will," she told him, "and remember I love you, sweetie." At that Scott told her he loved her also and they hung up and went their separate ways.

Tiffany decided to get a sub and take it back to her room. She wanted to avoid the crowds and to be alone.

At work the next day Tiffany greeted Hope, but what she saw was rather disturbing. She walked in and saw her friend shooting up with heroin and when she saw her Hope didn't see her right away, but she looked up just as she pulled the needle out of her arm and she looked astonished when she saw the look on Tiffany's face. Tiffany stood staring at her friend in disbelief. "Don't say a word," Hope told her, "and promise not to tell anyone."

"I wasn't going to, it's just this is all so disturbing to me. I didn't know you were using heroin. I don't even know where to start to say anything," Tiffany told her friend. After that Tiffany felt badly for her friend.

"How old are you, Hope?" Tiffany asked, trying to change the subject.

"I'm forty-two years old and I have two daughters, ages one and three."

"I didn't know that," Tiffany said. "You actually don't look much older than a thirty-year-old woman," Tiffany said.

"Yeah, a lot of people tell me I look younger than I am. With two daughters sometimes I feel older than I am though," Hope told her friend. "How old are you, Tiffany?" Hope asked trying to make conversation.

"I'm twenty-four and I have a boyfriend Scott who is back in California waiting for me."

"I've never been married and the father of my kids took off with another woman. I have a new boyfriend, but he doesn't care for the kids crying all the time. It makes it pretty rough a lot of the time. I do love him, he just seems hard to deal with."

"That's too bad that you have to support your two daughters on your own," Tiffany told her friend.

"Yeah, unfortunately some men are like that and I just happened to get a lemon," Hope said unhappily.

The rest of the day was rather busy but Tiffany had her undivided attention on her friend's problem. When Scott called her at the end of the day and she explained everything to him he agreed as well that it was unfortunate for Hope and her two daughters.

"I would never do anything like that to you, sweetheart," Scott told her with a sound of concern in his voice. "I think men should be more responsible for their actions."

"Europe is different and it gives me a change of scenery, but I'm going to be just as happy to return home and be with you and spend Christmas with my loved ones," Tiffany said. She sounded kind of sad as she was telling him all about everything that was bothering her and he kind of smiled to himself at her image and how she probably looked as she was saying it.

"How's your dad doing?" Tiffany asked. "Have you heard anything else about him?"

"No nothing new. I did talk to my mom last night and he's stable as of right now and hanging in there, but he might have to have another operation and he'll definitely have to have chemo if he does pull through."

"Well I'll talk to you tomorrow," Scott told her.

"What are you gonna do on your day off there in Europe?" Scott asked.

"I think I'm gonna do some Christmas shopping," she told him.

"Well have fun and call at the end of the day or any time if you need anything," Scott said.

"You know I always need something, sweetie," Tiffany said.

After Tiffany hung up she ordered room service and after she ate she decided to go to the park and just take a peaceful walk to clear her head and to enjoy herself a little. The weather was gorgeous and as Tiffany sat on a park bench she watched a couple of children playing and their mother was watching them and she spoke to Tiffany. At the end of the day Tiffany went back to the hotel room and she slept till morning.

Sunday was quiet but enjoyable and Tiffany spent the day Christmas shopping as she told Scott she would. She had bought many things and she had many treasures at the day's end. When she got back to her room she phoned Scott as she said she would.

"Did you go Christmas shopping today?" Scott asked.

"Yeah, I did," she said smiling as she said it.

"Did you buy lots?" Scott asked.

"Yeah, I bought several things," she told him. "How did your day go?" she asked.

"It was kind of lonely but I got through it," he told her. He sounded like he was pouting as he was talking to her. "It was good to hear your voice, Tiffany," Scott told her just before she hung up the phone.

"Yeah, I feel the same say, Scott," she told him.

The next day and the whole week were very busy and it was Sunday again. Tiffany was talking to Scott and he told her his dad was out of the hospital but things weren't looking good for him. "He may not make it," Scott told her.

"I'm sorry, Scott, but I don't know what to say or do," she said with a sound of concern in her voice.

"There's nothing you can say or do, baby," Scott told her.

"One more week and counting," Scott said, "and you'll be home."

"Yeah, that's right," she said, "Just in time for the holidays."

"Well I guess I'll let you go," he told her and she said the same thing on her end of the line.

The following week had its ups and downs and Tiffany saw her friend using heroin and she felt bad for her. She told Scott all about it, but that was all she could do and it made her feel helpless as far as actually helping her. By Saturday she was on the plan flying home and it felt good when she was finally back in familiar territory.

"I'm glad you're back home, sweetheart," Scott said when she called him. "Things are finally settling down here at the agency."

"That's good," Tiffany said.

"I'm gonna take the holidays off and spend them with you, baby," he told her. "I missed you so much."

"Sounds good to me," she said.

"I guess Christmas is this Wednesday," Tiffany said. "The next couple days are gonna go by quickly," she said.

"We'll go Christmas shopping for the rest of our gifts," Scott told her.

"Sounds good to me," she said.

The days in between were spent Christmas shopping and Christmas was spent at Tiffany's parents as planned. Everyone talked and Christmas dinner was enjoyable and festive and interesting. Rachel and Tiffany and Tracy talked and Rachael went on about her pregnancy, as expected she would. It was a day of opening gifts and just being around friends and family. At day's end the snow was falling as everyone left Tiffany's parent's house and Tracy thanked everyone for coming.

"It feels like Christmas," Scott said as they walked out into the snowflakes and the two of them danced in the snow. "I love you so much," Scott told her.

As they went to bed that night they kissed and when they fell asleep Scott knew in his heart that he had to make Tiffany his wife forever.

Chapter 19

The next day just the day after Christmas brought bad news for Scott. His mom called and told him his dad died overnight in his sleep.

"At least he didn't suffer a lot," Tiffany told him.

"Yeah, that is true, I didn't want him to suffer," Scott told her.

The day of the funeral was kind of bleak as funerals are and Scott had tears in his eyes as he looked at his dad. There were a lot of people at the funeral home that day and in the evening they held a dinner at Scott's mom's place. A lot of women brought covered dishes to show their gratitude and concern. Scott didn't say much throughout dinner. He was unduly quiet and Tiffany understood. She just tried her best to comfort him as much as possible. He was so young, some of the people were saying. It's too bad, others were saying.

"I'm sorry, Scott," was all Tiffany could say.

At the end of the day Scott was still extremely quiet but he lightened up when they got in bed and he seemed more at ease. They had excellent sex as they always did and the two of them had sex over and over.

"I'm so happy you're in my life, Tiffany. You mean the world to me and I don't know what I'd do without you, baby," he told her.

What she didn't know was he wanted to ask her to marry him again. He had to come to grips on his dad's passing and he knew in his heart of hearts that he was going to ask her again very soon to marry him. She wanted to ask him if there was something wrong but she already knew what was bothering him.

After he had sex that night he seemed very cold, like he didn't want to be bothered by her. He had never been this way before. She just dismissed it like it was because of his dad's passing. In the morning he seemed much better like a weight was lifted off his shoulders. He was open again and talking and he seemed happier than he had the night before.

"I truly love you, Tiffany," he said as they were making love.

"I guess tomorrow is New Year's Day," Tiffany said with a smile.

"Yeah, what do you say we take a drive to the city. We'll celebrate with champagne and the works. After all, what is New Year's Day without alcohol and celebration?" Scott asked.

"Oh I agree fully," she laughed.

They drove to the city in the morning and they stopped and had lunch before going to their room. They had a Jacuzzi in their room and a big poster bed, which they put to good use immediately.

"You make like so fun," Tiffany told Scott.

"Yeah, and you make my life fun, exciting, romantic, mysterious, and very happy and I don't know what I'd do without you in my life," and he wanted to add, *Will you marry me, baby?*

"I'm not sure about the mysterious part of your statement," she teased.

"Oh, is that right, you mysterious woman you," he said as he found a ticklish spot on her body and he began tickling her as she laughed and they began to make love. "You are a wonderful woman, an excellent love, and you know how to pleasure and please a man, baby, because when we're together in bed I couldn't ask for any more love if I wanted to," he told her.

"Oh you say the nicest, sweetest, most wonderful amazing things, Scott," she said as she kissed him and they made hot passionate love again and they lay spent. They spent the day making love and soaking in the Jacuzzi.

"Let's go to the bar," Scott said as it was later in the day and he wanted to bring in the New Year on the right track.

Tiffany had mixed drinks and Scott had beer and while they were there they danced and listened to the DJ and they had a wonderful time together. It was after midnight when they got back to their room. The two of them engaged in sex and they wanted each other so badly they made love again and again and fell asleep in each other's arms and slept till morning. When they awoke they made love and then they ordered room service and Scott said he was taking off till Monday and Tiffany said she was as well.

"We have four days, what do you say we go to Disney World California?"

"That would be a great idea, Scott," Tiffany said as she hugged him and they made love once more.

"Being with you all the time makes work really seem dull," Scott told her as they kissed and then they showered and dressed and went to get clothes to stay away for a few days.

Tiffany and Scott packed and they were off again and they arrived at Disney World later that day. They rode rides and saw some of the shows and the next day they did the same as the two of them enjoyed their time together.

"I don't want our time to end, Tiffany. My time with you goes way too fast anyway. I don't want to be without you."

Then he had to fight back the urge to ask her to marry him again.

She kind of sensed what he wanted to say and it made her feel defensive. She still was unsure if she wanted a commitment and she really didn't know why. She kind of changed the subject rather abruptly. All Scott could do was shake his head in dismay and wonder what the problem was. As far as he was concerned they should get married and maybe he thought they ought to be married already so what was the big deal? He asked himself. Why was she so scared? Or was she scared, was it something else that seemed to be bothering her? It all seemed upsetting to him and once again he tried to put it out of his mind. He was thinking to himself that he had to get her to realize that life was short, after all he thought, look what happened to his dad.

"Is there something bothering you?" she asked with a look of innocence and he smiled at her as she said it.

"Yeah I have a lot on my mind," he said, "and the main one is you," he was smiling as he said it.

"I do love you, Scott," she said grinning.

At day's end the two of them had dinner at a very fancy, extravagant, elegant restaurant.

"I could get used to this," Scott told her smiling as he was saying it.

"Yeah, so could I," she said. "I wish we could do this every day."

"Yeah, do so I, but I'd be completely broke," he said, smiling as he said it. "Well, I guess we'll be going back home tomorrow," Scott said.

"Yeah, unfortunately," she told him. "Back to the old grind again," he said and she said, "Don't remind me." He was laughing at her comments and she was laughing as well.

When they got back to the hotel room they made love over and over and they slept till morning. In the morning they awoke and made love first and then they showered and they were heading home within a few hours. Scott left her at her doorstep as he kissed her and he told her he'd see her in the morning. The two of them went their separate ways once more and Scott knew in his heart that he would ask her to marry him again real soon.

Chapter 20

The New Year was off with a bang and everyone was trying to get used to the fact that it was a new year already.

"I'm still writing the old year's date on everything," Scott told Tiffany when he talked to her.

"Yeah, you and me both," she said with laughter in her voice. "I think that's true with a lot of people," she told him and he agreed.

"How would you like to go to Venice, Italy, on Valentine's Day?" Scott asked.

"I would love to go," she told him with a sound of excitement.

"Plan on going then," he told her.

"I'll have to start packing now," she said. "How long are we going for?" she asked.

"Probably a month or so," he said. He figured that he would ask her to marry him while they were there. The days in January were short but they went by somewhat quickly and they were into February before long.

Tiffany and Scott spent all the time together that they possibly could and February Fourteenth was right around the corner.

"Are you all packed and ready to go, baby?" Scott asked with a smile.

"As a matter of fact I am," she told him.

"That's a big surprise," he joked with her as she said it, and she laughed.

"One thing about you, Scott, is that you make life fun."

"I'm glad you think so, baby doll," he told her.

Scott spent the night at Tiffany's and the day after they were leaving for Italy. They had wine to drink and pizza and they had on a good movie they both seemed to enjoy. Scott told Tiffany that he talked to his mother and he said that she said it was lonely without his dad.

"Your mom is young enough, she could find another man," Tiffany told him.

"Yeah, as a matter of fact she even said about that already," Scott said. "My mom is only fifty years old."

"Yeah, that is young yet," Tiffany said, "She's bound to find someone else at her age. It's understandable that she would be lonely," Tiffany told Scott.

The two of them drank several glasses of wine and they were feeling pretty good and they made love several times and fell asleep together and they slept till morning when they made love again. Scott had packed the car the night before.

The two of them made love in the shower and Scott was telling her that she had better get used to it as she was in store for more while they were in Italy.

"Oh, I am really?" she asked in a teasing manner.

As the two of them dressed Scott remarked how good Tiffany looked. She had on jeans and a T-shirt and her long blond mane of golden hair was down and the way she had curled it made her look so young and innocent and gorgeous he longed for her again.

"You look so pretty standing there and so young I could make love to you again," he told her and she smiled a sly smile.

"We better get on the road before we end up in bed again," she told him and he laughed at her comment.

Once they got on the road they stopped for coffee and breakfast sandwiches. "We should be there later tonight if everything goes right," Scott said.

The trip was spent with Scott and Tiffany talking and there were two couples sitting in front and on their right side of the plane. The ones on their right side had a little girl who kept looking at Tiffany with interest.

"We're going to visit my grandma," the little girl told Tiffany.

"Oh that's good," Tiffany said.

"What's your name?" the little girl asked with a look of enthusiasm.

"My name's Tiffany and what's your name?" Tiffany asked.

"My name is Taylor," the little girl told her.

"That's a pretty name," Tiffany told her with a smile, and then she asked her how old she was.

"I'm a whole four years old," the little girl said, trying to sound much older than she was.

Tiffany laughed and said, "You're getting old then,"

The little girl kind of got quiet for a while and then she opened up and talked throughout the rest of the trip.

"She makes the trip interesting and livelier," Scott told Tiffany as they sat hand in hand.

"Yeah, she sure does," Tiffany remarked.

"You're a pretty lady," the little girl remarked with a big smile and Tiffany said, "Thank you, honey, you're a very pretty little girl." She had a dark black head of hair just like her mother's and she looked like her mother. Her hair was naturally curly and she was holding a baby doll.

"Does your doll have a name?" Tiffany asked.

"Yeah her name is Lisa," Taylor told her.

The little girl had on a very pretty pink dress with flowers on it and she had matching pink bows in her hair.

"You look like you could be a model," the little girl told Tiffany.

"I am a model," Tiffany told Taylor and she added, "I'm an actress as well."

Scott laughed as the two girls were talking. The little girl's mother and dad talked some as well, which added to the conversation and made the trip more interesting.

"I thought I saw your picture in the tabloids," the little girl's mother remarked as they were entwined in conversation.

Tiffany laughed at that and said, "News gets around very fast."

"Yeah, it sure does," the little girls mom said.

"I sometimes wish I were famous," the mother said.

"Your last name is Long, isn't it?" the mother added as they engaged in conversation.

"Yeah, it is," Tiffany said with a smile.

"You can't hide when you're famous," she added. "People will notice you wherever you go."

"I'm not exactly sure how that would feel," the mother said as they engaged in conversation.

"I'm a loan consultant at the First Federal Bank," the mother of the daughter told Tiffany. "It's probably not near as exciting as what you do."

"I wouldn't know that for sure," Tiffany said, "but I do know I enjoy modeling and I enjoy acting as much but there's a price to pay for being successful."

"Oh I would say that I agree with you on that instance."

"By the way my name is Laura," the mother of the little girl replied. "I wish I could be a model and an actress just to try it," she said.

"That would be a very good experience for you and I'm sure you would absolutely love the recognition and everything that goes along with it for a while, but the price you pay for success is sometimes greater than the benefits. A lot of people can't handle success very well," Tiffany told Laura. Tiffany said it with a look of sincerity.

"Oh I believe you're probably right about what you're telling me, but everyone always says the grass is greener on the other side," Laura told her friend.

Tiffany laughed at that and replied, "I have heard that statement many times."

"Yeah and the more you hear it the more it seems to be true," Laura added. Then she said, "A person doesn't know until you experience it yourself."

"Yes, I agree with you one hundred percent," Tiffany told Laura.

The two of them had a very good conversation and they were told that the plane was due to make a landing.

"It was nice meeting you," Laura told Tiffany.

"Yeah, it was nice talking to you as well," Tiffany told her, before they got off the plane.

The couple's little girl was waving to Tiffany as they said their goodbyes.

"They made the trip go by quickly," Scott told Tiffany.

"Yeah, they surely did," Tiffany told Scott as they got off the plane.

"Now to get our bearing," Scott said as he tried to figure out where to go next.

The weather was beautiful there as it was sunny and warm and the two of them made their way to a taxicab and Scott flagged him down.

"Where to?" the taxi cab driver asked.

"Take us to the tourist center," Scott told him. He figured that would be the best place to go to get information and to know better where everything was located. It was the first time either of them had been to Italy.

"It's beautiful here," Tiffany told Scott.

"Yeah, I agree that is," Scott replied.

It was two o'clock in the afternoon and the two of them stopped at a little restaurant for something to eat.

"I feel like eating something Italian," Tiffany told Scott.

"Yeah you and me both," Scott told her.

Tiffany picked out a lasagna dinner and Scott picked out a spaghetti dinner and the two of them had a light wine to drink.

"I wish we could just spend our time vacationing," Scott said.

"Yeah, same here," Tiffany said with a smile. "The time goes quicker when you get to do what you enjoy doing," she told Scott with a small smile as she said it.

"Do you want to go for a ride up the river after we get done eating here?" Scott asked.

"Yeah, I would absolutely enjoy doing that for the rest of the afternoon," she told Scott.

"Tomorrow we'll go to see the Leaning Twoer of Pisa," Scott said. "We can go to some of the shops as well," Scott told her.

"Yeah I do want to do some shopping while we are here. We may never come back here again," she told Scott.

"You never know," he said. "You have to enjoy your time while you are here and make it count for something," Scott said.

"Oh I agree with you about that," Tiffany told Scott.

After they ate the two of them rented a canoe and they floated down the river in the canoe. "This is absolutely relaxing and romantic as well," Tiffany told Scott and he agreed as much.

"I wish we could do this kind of stuff more often," Scott told her. He smiles as he said it and the two of them kissed at that.

It was moonlit on the water and Scott and Tiffany looked up at the same time and together they saw a shooting star. At that moment Scott turned to Tiffany and he asked the question he had longed to ask and had planned to ask on this trip anyway. He asked at that moment as he looked longingly into her eyes. "Tiffany, will you marry me?"

She hesitated for a little bit and then she answered, "Yes, yes, I will marry you."

She kissed and hugged him at that and he replied, "I think I see stars," and then he added, "I was so afraid you'd say no. I was gonna ask you on this trip anyway and that was perfect timing with the falling star and this setting and everything."

She agreed as she laughed with glee. "It was perfect timing and this is such a romantic place."

The two of them sat side by side talking, kissing, and hugging.

"I love you more and more," and he put the ring on her finger as he was saying it. "You completely stole my heart by saying yes. I'm going to make you the best husband possible, baby. I won't let you down, sweetheart," he told her. "You made me a very happy man by saying yes," Scott told her.

"I'm happy if you're happy," she told him smiling as she said it and he could see her face in the moonlight. She was smiling at him and he was absolutely feeling like a lucky man. They could hear music playing in the background and the whole scene was romantic and spelled love. It was later when they pulled the boat over and got out and the two of them walked arm in arm back to their room that Scott cupped his hands over her breasts and he pulled her on the bed and at that he undressed her and she undressed him and they made love.

"I'm a happy, lucky man tonight, Tiffany, and it's all because of you, my love." He looked at her beaming and she was smiling back at him as he was saying it.

"Well whether you know it or not I feel like a lucky woman knowing you finally asked me to marry you." They made love a couple more times and they fell asleep in each other's arms satisfied and happy and they hardly moved till morning.

"Oh baby, how do I love you?" Scott asked first thing in the morning. He was feeling overwhelmed with pleasure and he thought to himself that he wouldn't get over it for the rest of his life or at least for a long, long time.

They made love first thing in the morning and Tiffany made coffee and cinnamon bagels for breakfast. She was standing in the nude as she was making breakfast and Scott was thinking to himself that this was a wonderful life, especially now that she said yes for marriage. He felt like a very lucky man and she was a beautiful woman to say the least. "How could he be so lucky?" he asked himself over and over in his mind.

"What's in store for us today?" she asked smiling as she said it, wearing nothing but a smile.

"I was thinking about taking you sightseeing today," he told her as they began to make love in the kitchen first and then in bed, and once again in the shower.

"You're absolutely spoiling me with all this lovemaking and everything we're doing and everything we've done in the past," Tiffany told him as she dressed for the day.

"You look absolutely sultry and amazing," he told her as he was watching her dress.

"I love your choice of words," she remarked, smiling as she said it.

"Oh do you really, babe?" he asked looking somewhat boyish as he said it and she smiled to herself how cute he truly looked. She could see the little boy in Scott in many ways and that's what made her love him and want him more than ever and she left him know it in the way she loved him and in the way she made love to him. He showed her all the affection in the world when they were one together and she gave it all back to him when they made love. The two of them were very compatible and they complemented each other while they were out or at lunch or just out on the twon or regardless of what they were doing.

The two of them spent the day sightseeing as Scott said they would. They saw the Leaning Twoer of Pisa and they went through a couple of museums and they enjoyed the day to the fullest together. They stopped for dinner that night.

"I took a lot of pictures today," Scott told Tiffany at the end of the day. "I hope you had a good time," Scott said once they got back to the motel room.

"Yes I did," he said, "I always have a good time when I'm with you and we're together."

"The time goes all too quickly though when we're together," Scott said and Tiffany agreed with him about that statement.

They picked out a god movie that night to watch before they fell asleep. The two of them made love several times and afterwards they lay spent in each other's arms, and they slept till morning.

In the morning they made love a couple times first and they showered and as they dressed Scott remarked that Tiffany looked absolutely gorgeous in the morning without a trace of makeup on and her hair was undone and at that he sat smiling at her. He watched her as she put on her makeup and he said "I don't know why you even bother to put that one. You're pretty without it, baby."

"I love your comments," she told him and she was smiling as she said it.

They stopped for a bite to eat and Scott asked her what she wanted to do for the day.

"What are my choices?" she asked with a curious look.

"I don't know," he said and he added, "we'll probably have to feel our way though."

It turned out that they rented a boat and they spent the day sailing on the water. It was almost dark when they got out of the water and back on shore. They ate at a little pizza lace and it was as if the two of them had almost forgotten that they had obligations and such. "It's easy to leave all your work behind you when you're having so much fun," Scott beamed and Tiffany agreed fully.

"This being here is absolutely spoiling me," she said.

"Do you really think so?" Scott asked and he added, "I hope it is. I love to spoil you."

"Oh do you really," she teased.

"You know I do, sweetheart," Scott told her smiling with satisfaction as he said it.

"Tomorrow I'll take you shopping," he told her and she agreed that would be a good idea.

"That pizza here is very good," Tiffany said and Scott agreed that he liked it just as much. At the day's end Scott and Tiffany walked hand in hand back to the hotel and once inside they made love first in bed and once in the Jacuzzi.

"I can get used to this," Scott told her with a big grin and she was smiling up at him as well and he remarked about how nice the ring looked on her finger and he told her at the same time that she made him a happy man.

"Oh do I make you a happy man?" she asked with a big grin.

"Yes, baby, yes, you certainly do," he said.

"That could be a good thing," she said sounding a little uncertain and she said it with a mischievous voice.

"You're absolutely the love of my life, Tiffany, and I'll do everything I can possibly do to make you happy," he told her. "I'll never let you down and I'll always try to be here for you, baby," he told her with a positive tone in his voice. "Remember one thing, Tiffany, life is what you make of it. You can go through life alone or you can choose to spend it with the one you love," he told her. "I want to spend my life with you, sweetheart. I chose you because I love you so much," he told her.

He hoped with the conversation at hand that she didn't have second thoughts and she wasn't about to change her mind and he thought that would be a complete letdown. He was also thinking to himself that he didn't think he could handle a situation like that.

The days in Venice, Italy, came and went too quickly and Tiffany and Scott did a lot of sightseeing and a lot of shopping as well as a lot of just plain enjoying themselves. They did a lot of boating also and they had only one more day to go.

"It only figures that our time here would be over," Tiffany said sounding somewhat sad and disappointed.

"Yeah I agree with you, baby," Scott told her sounding somewhat sad as well.

"Oh well, that's life for you," Tiffany said.

On their last day there they took a trolley car throughout the city and they had a wonderful time. They saw a lot of scenery as they rode along and they had a very enjoyable time as well. The two of them sat and Scott had his arm around Tiffany's shoulder and they kissed spontaneously. Scott was thinking to himself that he was a very lucky man to have Tiffany in his life. Now they had a wedding to go through, he thought to himself. He also was thinking to himself that he didn't want her to back out of the engagement or to get cold feet about the wedding and all.

"What do you say we have a December wedding?" Scott asked.

"That sounds a little sudden to me," she told him.

He didn't like what he was hearing and he asked her to at least think about it. She said she would think about it, which satisfied him for the time being. She thought he was getting a little pushy to say the least but she didn't want to push the issue so she kept quiet for the time being.

"Well tomorrow we go back home," Scott said sounding somewhat sad that their vacation was over.

"Yeah," she told him, "I don't even like to think about that."

"Cheer up, baby," Scott said with a smile. "It isn't the end of the world."

It was later when they got off the trolley and went back to their room. The two of them ordered pizza and they took it back to their room as they wanted to spend their last night alone together. After they ate, they undressed one another and they made love. Scott kept saying how much he loved her and he added again that he was happy she accepted the engagement ring. She was starting to think that might have been a mistake as she was beginning to have doubts. She wanted to marry him in a way, but in her own mind she had questions. Questions like, did she really want to be tied down? Did she want to get married at such a young age? The only thing she was sure of was that she didn't want to upset him further. Maybe she should have put him off for a while longer, she was thinking to herself. On the other hand, what was she so afraid of and why? Oh well, she thought, I already said yes. Maybe she was afraid he'd leave her if she had said no. Whatever the case was she had already said yes and for now she was willing to go through with the marriage. After all, she thought the situation, the timing, the place, everything was so romantic and all that along with the falling star, maybe it was meant to be.

"What were you thinking just now?" Scott inquired. She seemed focused on something and she was unduly quiet. It was like he could read her mind or something of that nature.

"Oh nothing," she said rather quickly, "just that I'm sad our vacation is over already."

"I'm sorry about that as well," he told her. Then he added, "We'll take another vacation very soon."

The two of them engaged in sex and romance throughout the night and neither of them wanted it to end so soon. Morning came all too soon for both of their likings and they were both sad to see their vacation end.

"Vacations are never long enough," Scott said.

"I agree with you," Tiffany told him.

"Well we have a plane to catch this morning," Scott said.

"Yeah unfortunately," Tiffany said looking sad as she said it and Scott could read her like a book as she said it.

"I'm sorry our vacation is over, baby," Scott said trying to sound reassuring. "I don't like it either," he told her.

The two of them were packed and heading twoard the airport before very long. At the terminal it was busy, but the trip was kind of dull and neither Scott nor Tiffany said much. Once the plane landed and they were back in familiar territory they decided to stop and get something to eat. The two of them decided to have Mexican food for a little something different. At the end of the day Scott spent the night at Tiffany's place. They made love once but their lovemaking wasn't quite what it had been as it wasn't as intense, and Scott was kind of puzzled as to why that was. When they awoke the next day they made love and Tiffany made breakfast. She made blueberry pancakes and sausage and coffee and Scott suggested they spend the day just doing nothing, but enjoying one another's company.

"Sounds good to me," she said as she was making breakfast. "Sometime it's good to have the day to yourself with no obligations," Tiffany told Scott.

The two of them spent the day watching movies and enjoying each other's company. At the end of the day they had pizza delivered and when Scott left he kissed Tiffany and told her he hoped she had had a good time overall, and she agreed that she did.

"I'll see you tomorrow at work," Scott said just as he was walking to his car and she stood watching him out her window as he drove away.

Chapter 21

The next day at work started out to be a busy one for Tiffany. For one thing she woke up late and she arrived at work a little late and the day started out with a big bang and as she walked through the door at work Scott greeted her as usual.

"Did you wake up a little late this morning, Tiffany?" Scott asked with a smile.

"Yeah, don't say anything about it," she told him.

"I almost did too," he said in order to cheer her up.

She kind of smiled as he said it and he was laughing as well. "Vacations have a way of doing that to a person," Scott said to reassure her. "They have a way of making a person forget that they have obligations," Scott said.

"Don't remind me of vacations, especially since ours is over," she said trying to sound persuasive and talk him into another vacation very soon.

"Don't sweat the small stuff sweetheart as I have a trip for you in London in exactly two weeks. It is for a movie this time and I think I can break away this time and possibly go with you, but I'm not exactly sure."

That night after work Scott and Tiffany went out for dinner and Scott kissed Tiffany at her door and he told her that they had a lot to do the next day so he didn't stay.

It was already the middle of March and it felt like it to Tiffany, as she felt like the wind just about swept her off her feet on her way to work the next day. The next few days at work went by somewhat quickly and it was the end of the week already.

"Thank goodness it's Friday," Scott said at the end of the day and he had already promised to take Tiffany out to dinner and a movie. "I found out that I can't go to London with you, baby," Scott told her.

"Too much work at the agency for you, is that why?" she asked.

"Yeah, you could say that," Scott replied.

"I'm getting packed already," she told him. "I think I have some ideas of my own."

"Oh really, like what?" Scott asked.

"I'm kind of thinking about designing my own handbags and outerwear and undergarments," she told him.

"Oh really?" he asked, and he added, "That sounds very interesting. You are a very talented, smart, sexy, lovely, beautiful woman, and I love you to my very core," Scott told her.

"I'm thinking about opening up my own store by summer or possibly by fall," she told Scott with a look that spelled complete success. "That little leather shop on Main Street is due to close up and go out of business and I'm gonna buy it when it does."

"You are going to make me a very happy when we get married in December," Scott told her.

At that Tiffany was thinking to herself that she was uncertain about the wedding plans but she continued to let Scott persuade her. Maybe she should be honest with Scott and tell him how she felt, better yet maybe she should be honest with herself. She thought at that that she was an absolutely pushover. She left him take advantage of her that way. He did and he was going to for the rest of her life if she let him. How stupid can I be? she asked herself over and over in her own mind. If she wasn't happy getting married now, how could she possibly be happy after they got married? She was willing to go through with the marriage just to keep peace with Scott. She told herself that wasn't a reason, but she was letting it happen regardless. She was gonna go through with the marriage in hopes that it make both of them happy.

She started thinking of making wedding plans as she knew December was only nine months away and that would go by quickly.

"Why don't we get married in a tropical paradise?" Scott suggested and then he added, "Just the two of us."

"That would work for me as well," she told him, "as that would eliminate a lot of the hassle. Do you want to get married in Hawaii?" Tiffany asked and Scott agreed that would be a good place to get married as well.

"It sounds very romantic to me," Tiffany told him and Scott agreed. "We could get married there and just invite immediate family and a few friends," Tiffany said.

"Yeah, that would simplify things and make a lot less hassle for both of us," Scott told her. After much consideration that's what the two of them decided they'd do.

"All I need to do at that rate is pick out a wedding dress and decide who to invite," Tiffany said. "That makes me happy as I know how hectic it can be making wedding preparations," Tiffany told him looking happy with her final decision.

They went out that night and saw a good movie and they went to dinner and the two of them had a wonderful time and at the end of the day Scott stayed at Tiffany's place as he did many times before. They made love and slept like babies together till morning. In the morning they made love and Tiffany made eggs and toast and bacon and Scott and her kissed and Scott pulled her close to him and patted her behind and the two of them wound up in bed again.

"I'm thinking about taking you to the beach today, baby," Scott told her. "What do you say about that?" he asked.

"Sounds like a good idea, I would like to spend the day at the beach," she told him wearing nothing but a smile.

"I could get used to you wearing nothing," Scott said and the two of them wound up making love again and then once more in the shower.

As Tiffany dressed Scott kept remarking about how he'd like to take her to bed and ravish her again. Tiffany said, "You'd better not or we'll never leave."

"That might be a good thing," Scott told her.

"Oh, do you really think so?" she asked.

"Yeah, I know so," he told her laughing as he said it.

"Men," she said, "you can't live with them and you can't live without them."

"I was thinking the same thing about women," Scott said.

"Oh, were you really now?" she asking sounding amused.

"Yeah, as a matter of fact I was," he told her.

The two of them walked along the water hand in hand making conversation and then they stopped at the little snack shop for some pizza and ice cream. Around noon they rented a small boat and went sailing in the ocean.

"Let's get a motel room up the coast and spend the night there," Scott suggested.

"That would be a very good idea," Tiffany agreed with Scott as she smiled back at him.

"Look over there, Scott," Tiffany said in an unusual tone of voice. Then she asked if he saw the same thing she saw.

"Yeah," he said, "there's something in the water."

"What in the world is it?" Tiffany asked sounding panicked.

"I don't know for sure, it looks like a spool of dolphins or on the other hand it could be a shark," Scott told her.

"We'd better paddle back to shore just to be on the safe side," Scott said.

Tiffany said she agreed fully that they'd better paddle back to shore. As they paddled out of the water they got closer to shore. They were getting tired but they were still going with every last little bit of strength they could muster up. By then others who were in the water were getting out as well.

"I'm getting tired," Tiffany said as she paddled her way out of the water.

"You're doing a good job," Scott told her. "Keep up the good work."

"It looks like dolphins," the one guy said as they all made their way back to shore.

Tiffany breathed a huge sigh of relief as he said it, hoping he was right.

"It feels good to see the sand," Scott said and Tiffany agreed fully.

"You almost feel like kissing the ground you walk on after a scare like that," Tiffany said.

"Yeah, I believe you're right," Scott replied.

Everyone was relieved to find out that it was dolphins and not sharks.

"That was scary enough, it almost makes it so you don't want to go back into the water," Tiffany said.

"I agree with you one hundred percent," Scott said sounding relieved that they were finally safe and back on shore.

After they got their bearings back the two of them decided to get something to eat. Tiffany said she wanted to go to the open-pit barbeque restaurant. Scott agreed that was a good idea as well.

Scott filled up on barbeque ribs and fries and Tiffany had barbeque chicken breasts and fries. For dessert they had apple dumplings with ice cream.

"You could gain a lot of weight eating like this," Tiffany said.

"Yeah, it could certainly throw your diet out of whack," Scott said laughing.

Once back at the hotel Scott found a good movie to watch and he made popcorn.

"You can't watch a movie and not have popcorn to go with it," Scott replied.

The two of them cuddled up on the sofa. "This is cozy being here with you," Tiffany told him.

"Oh, I agree," Scott said.

It wasn't long till they had their clothes off and they were making love. First on the sofa and then in the bed. The two of them made love first thing in the morning and they ordered room service, and after they ate they made love again and again in the shower. While Tiffany dressed Scott was telling her that he wanted her again and she remarked that they would never get out the door.

"I was going to take you shopping to some of the various stores and boutiques," Scott told her smiling as he said it. He knew how to win her over as he knew a lot of her likes and dislikes.

"Do you want to bump the wedding up and make it in June?" Scott asked smiling sheepishly.

Tiffany thought about it and she answered, "Yeah that wouldn't be such a bad idea after all."

Scott was rather surprised and happy by her answer. By then they had told their parents and as it turned out Scott's mother was all for the wedding and Tiffany's parents were all for it as well.

"Let's have the wedding here in California," Tiffany suggested.

"Yeah, we really don't have much time to make plans and I've always heard simple weddings are best," Scott said.

"Let's let it at that as I don't want to change our plans again," Scott said and Tiffany agreed.

"We're working pretty fast, but when you love each other you can't work fast enough," Scott said with a big grin.

"About next I'll be pregnant," Tiffany said and she added, "as fast as we're working."

Scott laughed at her comment and said, "I'd love to make you pregnant."

"I promise you that I'll always take care of you, baby," Scott told her.

"We'll have the wedding here at my parents home in San Francisco."

"Sounds good to me," Scott told her and the two of them stopped at the various boutiques and shops along the way. Tiffany was looking at wedding dresses and shoes and as she did she got several ideas and some dresses she liked better than others. The two of them stopped at Tiffany's parent's place t:woard the end of the day and Scott and Tiffany told them about deciding to move the wedding to June instead of December. Tiffany's mom said she thought they should have three hundred guess or more and Tiffany said they were going to make it a simple wedding with only one hundred guests and Tiffany decided on one hundred and fifty guests finally to please her mom and herself finally. Scott and Tiffany's dad washed the movie in the TV room and didn't say a whole lot about it. They left the two women argue it out.

Tiffany's mom thought she should wear a short dress and Tiffany agreed with her that would be a good idea as well. In other ways she felt like telling her mother that it was her day and she would make her own decisions. By the time David remarked, "We men will let the women hash out the wedding plans. We're better off to just stay out of it and mind our own business."

Scott laughed and told David he agreed with him totally. One thing Scott sensed was that both her parents seemed to like him and that made him very much at ease. The four of them talked long into the night and before the two kids left Tracy thanked them for coming.

"I'm glad we get along so well with your parents," Scott said after the two of them were in his car and backing out the driveway. Tracy stood in the doorway waving as their car disappeared out the driveway.

"That went well," Scott said as they drove away.

"Oh, do you think so?" and then she added, "Maybe in your mind it did."

Scott laughed at her comment and asked, "What was that statement about?"

"My mom's fine as long as everything is her way."

"I hadn't noticed that about her."

"Yeah, and you didn't live with her for all those years like I did."

"This is very true," Scott told her. "Cheer up, baby," he said, "as all this will be over in a few short months and you'll be the new Mrs. Tiffany Barlow."

"Tiffany Barlow," she said, "I like the name and the sound of it."

"That's good as you'll be using it for the rest of your life," He told her.

"Tomorrow let's go to my mom's house and tell her the good news of moving our marriage up." Tiffany agreed that would be a good idea.

"Let's go to the South of France for our honeymoon," Scott said.

"Since we're getting married in June we can go on our honeymoon right away, which is a good thing," Scott told Tiffany.

"Yeah, I agree about that as well," Tiffany said. "If we would have waited till December I wouldn't have had time as it's very busy at the agency and with Christmas and all it makes it very unbalanced with all the shopping and all."

Once back at Tiffany's place the two of them made dinner. Scott barbequed the chicken and Tiffany made a salad and baked potatoes and they had ice cream with chocolate sauce for dessert.

"I'm happy with our decision to get married sooner," Tiffany said as she set the table.

"I hope so," Scott replied.

After they finished eating they made love and they lay together spent and they slept till morning. Then they made love as they awoke. On their way to Scott's mom's the next day Tiffany discussed wedding plans.

"I hope your mom agreed to us getting married sooner."

"She's not that hard to please," Scott said, "and besides that she really likes you, which is a good thing to start with."

"Yeah I agree with you there, and I like your mom also."

Once the two of them got to Scott's mom's she invited them in and they told her their news. She was very understandable and she asked how many people were gonna be there. They had sandwiches and soup, which his mom prepared and the two of them helped her. They talked about the wedding and other miscellaneous things and it was later in the day when the two of them left. They got back to Tiffany's around nine o'clock and this time Scott kissed her and left her at her door.

Chapter 22

The two months to follow were very hectic, what with the wedding and all. Scott and Tiffany spent as much time together as they possibly could. The wedding was only two days away. It was on Saturday, June the sixth, and Scott and Tiffany and the whole wedding party were about a nervous wreck.

"We should have just eloped," Tiffany told Scott, "then we wouldn't have to go through with this."

"A lot of people do, but I wanted to give you a traditional wedding, something we'll both remember. Besides that a lot of people elope because they have a shotgun situation," Scott told her.

"I do love you, Scott, and I hope this is all worth it."

"Oh, it is, babe, believe me it is," Scott said with a big smile.

The day of the wedding Scott was waiting in the front of the church with all the groomsmen and the best man. He was a little nervous to say the least. The maid of honor started walking down the aisle along with the flower girl and the ring bearer. The other bridesmaids followed and then everyone turned to see the bride as the organist started to play "Here Comes the Bride." Tiffany looked lovely. She had chosen a long taffeta dress with a long train and lace around the neckline and roses down the sleeves, a veil was covering her face and she had her golden blond hair in a braid wrapped around her head. Her makeup was done just so. She would have looked lovely without any makeup on, she always did as far as Scott was concerned and he had told her that many times. The preacher preached the sermon and Scott and Tiffany exchanged vows. The two of them put their rings on each other's fingers and the preacher introduced them as the new Mr. and Mrs. Barlow.

Pictures of the bride and groom, the bridal party, and Tiffany's parents and Scott's mother were taken. Afterwards all the people who wanted to go were invited to Tiffany's parent's place for a reception. They had a wonderful reception. The food was catered and they had a variety of meats and potatoes and salads and desserts and fruits. They also had appetizers of all kinds. They had punch and mixed drinks and beer as well.

Tiffany changed into more comfortable clothing after the party started and Scott took off his suit jacket. Tiffany put on a pair of white jeans and a navy blue top. Scott and a bunch of the other guys were drinking beer and Tiffany and her friends were drinking mixed drinks. There was a band and folks were dancing. Tiffany danced with her father and Scott danced with his mother. The bride and groom danced together and then they danced with others. They also had a donation where man paid to dance with the bride. Everyone was talking and laughing at the various jokes that the others were telling.

Then the cake was cut and Scott gave Tiffany a piece and she in turn gave him a piece. It turned out to be a very good wedding and all the people seemed to be enjoying themselves.

Tiffany's mother thanked everyone for coming to the reception before they left.

That night Scott spent the night at Tiffany's place.

"How does it feel to be the new Mrs. Tiffany Barlow?" Scott asked as they entered the house.

"I love the sounds of it," she answered smiling back at him.

Scott pulled her close and kissed her sensuously and he started to undress her. She undressed him and they wound up on the carpet making love.

"So is this what happens to married people?" Tiffany asked with a cheerful laugh.

"You better believe it," Scott said as he made love.

They wound up in bed making love until they fell asleep in each other's arms. When they awoke they made love and Scott made Tiffany breakfast in bed and she joked that she could get used to that.

"It feels good being married," Tiffany said and she added, "I love it when you spoil me."

"I figure that our honeymoon will last about two months," Scott told her, "more or less," he added.

Once they ate they showered and dressed as they had a plane to catch. Tiffany had on blue jeans and a pink tunic and she had very little makeup on and her long blond hair hung down her back.

Getting on the plane was rather hectic as the airport was crowded and people were scurrying to catch their flights. The two of them looked like lovebirds as they stood at the terminal waiting to board the plane. Scott and Tiffany stood with their arms around each other embracing and kissing.

Once on the airplane Tiffany took a window seat and Scott sat on her right side. In front of them was a man and a woman and on their right side was two men who looked professional and business like. They looked like lawyers or accountants or something and Scott and Tiffany both agreed that was true as well.

"I kind of like a quiet flight like this," Scott told Tiffany.

"Yeah, I kind of agree with you." She was smiling back at him. They were given crackers and drinks about half way through the flight. When the flight was over and they had landed the two of them had to get their bearings. The first thing they did was stop at a café pizza snack shop.

"This is absolutely beautiful here and it makes a wonderful honeymoon," Tiffany told Scott and she added, "thank you for bringing me here."

"Oh I can't think of anything better than pleasing you," he said smiling pleased that he had impressed her.

"I'm gonna do my best to please you for the rest of our lives. I only want to make you happy, sweetie," he said.

"First thing we're gonna do is get a rental car so we have our freedom. I have several places we're gonna go while we're here and

I'm planning on taking this approximately a month or better," Scott told her.

The first thing they did after they ate was to go skiing in the Alps.

"I haven't been skiing since I was a girl," Tiffany said sounding pleased.

"At least you know how to ski," Scott told her. "I haven't been skiing since I was in college."

The two of them spent the day skiing. They had a very enjoyable time together. That night for dinner they chose pasta and they had garlic bread and wine to drink.

"Tomorrow we could go to the beaches here or we could go skiing again. I'm letting it up to you," Scott told her.

Once they got back to their hotel room Scott started to undress Tiffany and she pulled his shirt over his head and they were in bed in an instant making love. They slept like babies till morning in one another's arms. When they awoke in the morning they both felt the effects of the day before.

"Every single muscle and bone in my body aches," Tiffany said.

"Yeah, I feel the same way," Scott told her and he added, "I even have parts of me hurting that I didn't even know I had." The two of them laughed and they made love first and then they ordered room service for breakfast. They had a small, simple breakfast after which they made love again and then again in the shower. As Scott watched Tiffany dress he told her he wanted to take her to bed again and she laughed and asked him if that was all he thought about.

"Yeah, pretty much when I'm alone with you, baby," he said.

"I'm not sure but I guess that is a good thing," Tiffany told him smiling broadly as she said it.

"I love you so much, Tiffany Barlow," he said.

"I like the new name," she said.

"I hope so, baby doll, because it's your name for the rest of your life."

"Yeah and I couldn't be happier if I'd want to be," she said.

"I hope I make you happy," he told her. "Did you decide what you want to go today?" he asked.

"Yeah," she said, "as a matter of fact I did. I want to go skiing again today. That was so much fun yesterday I'm ready for more of the same," she told him.

"Good," he said, "then skiing it is."

Tiffany started down the slope and she fell and when she did she kind of twisted her ankle. Scott was right behind her and he was concerned that she might have broken her leg or her ankle or something.

"No," she said, "I twisted it is all. I think I'll be all right."

They skied the rest of the day and at the end of the day Scott nursed her ankle for her.

"What a stupid thing to do," she stated.

Her ankle was somewhat swollen and Scott put a cold pack on it in order to get the swelling down. Scott then ordered pizza and breadsticks and cinnamon sticks. The two of them ate pizza and watched a movie and afterwards they went to bed so Tiffany could rest her ankle. They didn't have sex as Scott didn't want to make her ankle any worse than it was already. Scott went to sleep that night feeling Tiffany's naked body next to his and he fell asleep dreaming about her.

"How's your ankle this morning?" Scott asked.

"It feels much better," she told him with a sleepy yawn.

"That's good," he said. "We'll have to do something less strenuous today," Scott told her.

The two of them made love as Scott pulled her closer to him. The two of them made love in the shower and as Tiffany dressed and did her hair and makeup Scott watched her and he acted like he wanted her again.

"You make my life fun and exciting and unpredictable," Tiffany said in a very upbeat tone.

"That's good as I wouldn't want to be boring and dull and lifeless. I'm hoping the rest of our lives are like this. I always want to please you and make you know you are wanted and don't you ever forget that I love you, baby," Scott added.

They stopped for breakfast before going to the beaches of Northeast France where they rented a sailboat and they were on the water the biggest part of the day. The two of them talked and kissed and hugged.

"If our lives together are going to be anything like this I'll always love you, Scott," Tiffany said smiling at him.

"Well I can't promise you that they'll always be this adventurous but I will do my best so I will," he said smiling broadly, pleased that she was impressed.

"There are quite a few boats out here today," Scott said and Tiffany agreed.

"It's a beautiful day to be out here in the water," Tiffany said.

"Yeah, it sure is," Scott agreed.

"I had a wonderful time today," Tiffany told Scott at the end of the day.

The two of them no more than got back to their room and they tore each others clothes off and they wound up in bed. They made love that night till they fell asleep in each others arms and the two of them slept till morning, barely moving.

The next few days were spent sightseeing. They sampled the many wines and champagne.

"There is so much to see and do here," Tiffany said.

"Yeah I know it's very interesting and very informative," Scott told Tiffany with a big smile. He was so amazed by the fact that she was so impressed by the honeymoon. The days to follow were spent seeing different statues and monuments and days lying on the beach and sailing and shopping. Tiffany went wild shopping and Scott remarked that she spent a small fortune. She had bought some Paris originals that she thought she just had to have.

"You make me so happy, baby," Tiffany said and Scott added, "I'm happy when you're happy."

Their days in Paris were winding down and they only had a few days to go.

"Where in the world did the time go?" Scott asked at the last of their honeymoon as they only had a few more days to go.

"It's hard to believe that a whole month has gone by," Tiffany said looking somewhat saddened.

"Oh I surely agree, sweetheart, but I'll do my very level best to make our lives adventurous in the future," Scott added. Tiffany knew he meant it by his sincerity when he was saying it. He looked somewhat boyish and she had to smile.

Before they left the hotel they made love and they ordered room service and they made love again and then again in the shower and as they dressed the two of them talked about what they wanted to do their last four days there. The two of them chose going to the opera and they went to the Rex movie theatre and that night they went to the Moulin Rouge nightclub. They danced at the La Loco, which was a huge disco and they had the time of their lives to say the least. They had France's finest food that night.

The next day they went to Franche-Comté to see the falls. They saw the striking Chapelle Notre Dame de Haut by Le Corbusier at Ronchamp and they saw many other museums along the way and many other different sights. Scott took a lot of pictures so they would have cherished memories of their honeymoon.

On their last day they decided to spend it at the beach as they were both pretty much satisfied that they had seen a lot, although they knew that there was so much more that they hadn't seen.

"You'd pretty much have to live here in order to see everything as this is a rather large area to cover," Scott told Tiffany as they lay on the beach and Scott had his arms around her.

"We've covered most all of it as we've been to Paris and France and Central France and the Alps and the South of France and Western France," Scott said.

"I hope you had a wonderful time, babe," Scott said.

"I want you to remember these moments for the rest of our lives," Scott told her.

The two of them took a walk up the beach hand in hand. They decided to stop at the little café and they ordered pizza for two.

"This honeymoon is really spoiling me," Tiffany said grinning. She had some pizza sauce on her chin and Scott was laughing.

"Are you saving that for later?" he asked jokingly.

"Oh shut up," she said, knowing how she must look. "Being here for a month is going to make going back to work seem dull and boring."

"I agree with you on that," Scott told her.

After they finished their pizza the two of them walked on up the coast and it was dark by the time they got back to their room. They took subs back to their room and Scott opened a bottle of champagne for their last night there.

"I'm gonna miss all of this as it's spoiling me badly," Tiffany said.

"I'm impressed that I've pleased you so much," Scott told her. "The bad part is now I'm gonna have to please you the rest of my life," he said joking with her.

"Well," she said, "I didn't know that was such as chore."

After they ate their subs and had a glass of champagne they took each others clothes off and they ended up in bed making love almost till midnight when Scott said they'd better get some sleep or they'd never make their flight the next day.

"That might be a good thing," Tiffany said smiling about the idea and all.

"What am I gonna do with you?" Scott asked.

"You should have thought about that before we got hitched," she told him.

"Ain't that the truth," he said and it wasn't long after that the two of them fell asleep dreaming of their time in Paris and when Scott awoke Tiffany was still sleeping. He had gone down the street and had come back with breakfast sandwiches and coffee. When he got back Tiffany was just getting out of bed.

"I brought you back breakfast in bed for the one I love," he said and before they had even eaten they made love first.

"I love everything you do for me, Scott."

"That's good as you have to put up with me for the rest of your life," he told her as they lay spent.

"Well, my love, we'd better get ready as we have a plane to catch."

"Yeah," she said, "I'm gonna miss all this once we're back home and back to our old routine."

"I promise you we'll make another vacation very soon. It might not be as extensive as this one or as long, but I'll think of something or should I say, we'll think of something."

They were dressed and headed out the door for the airport within an hour. Once on the plane the flight attendant seated the two of them. Tiffany read for a while and then she fell asleep about an hour later she had her head resting on Scott's shoulder. Scott fell asleep as well and when the two of them awoke the stewardess brought them a snack. It was midnight Los Angeles time when they arrived in California.

"It does feel good to be back at home," Scott said and Tiffany finally agreed.

"I guess you're right," she said looking rather sad that she had to face the facts again early Monday morning.

"We have two more days left of our honeymoon and I'm gonna make it count," Scott told Tiffany.

"Are you really now?" Tiffany asked.

"You better bet I am, doll baby," he said. They were pulling up to Tiffany's house as they were talking and they no more than got through the front door and they needed up in bed making love. In the morning Scott awoke and he made her breakfast and she was just getting out of bed as he entered the room.

"Breakfast smells good this morning," she told him.

"You look good this morning, my love," and Scott added, "I could eat you up."

"Is that right," she said and settled back into bed to see what he made. She thought he was a pretty good cook. He made eggs, hash browns, bacon, and toast and he even made cinnamon muffins.

"This is a pretty good breakfast," she told him wearing nothing but a smile.

"Yeah and I love it when I please you," he told her. "I'm happy you like it," he said. He smiled looking pleased that he satisfied her. The two of them spent the day talking and making love.

"I'm gonna put a down payment on that department store I said about," she told him.

"You mean the one where you're gonna design your own fashions?" he asked.

"Yeah that's right," she said.

"There's a lot of work involved but I think it'll be worth it in the long run," she remarked. "I'm gonna have my own line of handbags and coats and other various items."

"I'm sure that you'll be successful whatever you do, my love. You're truly an amazing woman and I'm very happy to be married to you."

"What are you gonna call your new store?" Scott asked.

"I'm not exactly sure yet, I have a few ideas but I'm not sure if I'm sold on them. I could go with Tiffany's collectables or on the other hand I was thinking about Candy Apple Fashions."

"Those are both good choices," Scott said.

"Can you think of any names?" Tiffany asked.

"Not really," he replied.

"You're not much help," she told him.

"I'll think of something between now and the time I'm ready to open my new store."

"Oh I'm quite certain you will," Scott said, "as you are a very talented woman and that is one of the reasons I love you so much."

"I'm glad about that or at least I think I'm glad about that," Tiffany said looking amused.

"You're a wonderful woman, you're pretty and talented as well."

"I'm happy you think so," she told Scott.

"Do you want to go out to see a movie and to dinner?" Scott asked.

"Yeah that would be nice," Tiffany said.

They made love and showered and dressed in blue jeans and T-shirts. The two of them picked out a movie that they both enjoyed. Afterwards they went out to dinner. They wrapped up the night making love.

"I can't seem to get enough of you, Tiffany," Scott said after they made love. They ended up making love again and they both knew one more day was all that they had left before they returned to work.

Sunday morning Tiffany woke up first and this time she made breakfast. She made cinnamon toast and coffee. The two of them showered and dressed. Tiffany put on a pair of short shorts and a T-shirt. They were going to the beach today, as they had decided earlier. They walked together hand in hand up the coast and Scott took her in his arms and hugged her tightly.

"I love you more and more everyday," he told her as he looked deep into her eyes.

"I love you too," she told him as they stood embracing in the hot California sunshine. They were so much in love and anyone could sense it as they watched them at a distance. The two of them decided to have steak dinners that night.

When they got back to Tiffany's place that night the first thing they did was make love and as they fell asleep that night they were happy and satisfied that they were married and they would spend the rest of their lives together.

Chapter 23

The two of them were sleeping so soundly neither of them heard the alarm go off early Monday morning. When they did get up it was approximately a half an hour later.

"Nothing like getting up on the wrong side of the bed and starting the week off with a bang," Scott said.

"Ain't that the truth," Tiffany moaned. "We have about enough time to take a shower and get to work."

The two of them showered and dressed and they were going out the door before long.

"We can go to work together today," Scott told Tiffany.

"Yeah talk about convenient," Tiffany said as they hurried to work.

They were almost to work and Scott pulled off at a donut shop and they got a dozen donuts and coffee for breakfast. Tiffany shared the donuts with her coworkers that morning when they arrived at work.

"You're running a little late this morning," Star told her as Tiffany go to her dressing room.

"Yeah honeymoons have a tendency to do that to a person," Tiffany told her friends with a humorous look.

"How did your honeymoon go?" Star inquired.

"It was absolutely great. I loved every minute of it," Tiffany said smiling. "I have a ton of pictures to share with all of you. We went skiing and I almost broke my ankle, that wasn't so great," Tiffany shared with her friends, "but the rest of it was fabulous."

"We were thinking about you and we missed you," Carried told her.

"I put a down payment on that vacant store across the street. I'm gonna buy it and open up my own line of fashions," Tiffany told her friends. "I'll have to hire people to run it."

"That sounds like a lot of extra work and hassle," the girls replied and Tiffany agreed but she said she liked a challenge.

The day was long and very tiring and both Tiffany and Scott were glad it was over and they were heading home. Scott made hamburgers and Tiffany made a salad for dinner that night. When they went to bed they were so exhausted they fell asleep immediately and they slept till morning and this time they got up when the alarm first went off.

Tiffany learned that day that she was going to London to do an acting show. She was going to be in a movie with stars like Jennifer Lopez and Halle Berry.

"It'll be October before I get back," she told Scott.

"I'm gonna have to stay here and run things here," he told her.

"It's going to make the rest of this year go by very rapidly," Scott said that night and Tiffany agreed. She had already started packing as she was leaving in one week. The rest of the week was busy and Friday night was upon them just like clock work. Tiffany's friends wanted her to go out with them to the bar but she refused them by saying she really wanted to spend her weekend with Scott. She told them she felt it was only right since she would be leaving for London in a few short days.

"It must be hell to be married," Star said. "After all you never do anything fun with us anymore."

"Well it depends how you look at it," Tiffany said. "I think marriage is an adventure."

"That's probably good that you look at it that way, otherwise you'd go nuts."

"Scott makes our marriage very interesting," Tiffany added.

"Wait till you have kids," Star said, "and you can no longer be a model and then you get fat."

"Oh gee thanks a lot for your vote of confidence," Tiffany said getting rather upset at what Star was telling her.

"Life is what you make of it," Carried added. "I have two kids and no husband to speak of and needless to say I'm raising my kids on my own and I'm super happy. I feel like I'm better off with no man running my life."

"Yeah you just might be better off," Star said. "Some men are very controlling and they act like babies who have to have their own way."

"Well Scott is different. We are very compatible and he always asks my opinion."

"Yeah and you two just got married. I mean you just got back from your honeymoon," Star replied.

"I'm not trying to please everyone, just myself," Tiffany said. "After all when you consider it that's all that matters."

"Well I guess I'm leaving on Monday morning first thing," Tiffany said, "so I won't see anything of this place for a month."

"Have a good trip," her friends all told her.

"Yeah I'll see all of you when I get back."

As Tiffany was walking out Scott was just finishing up putting props away and cleaning up.

"Well," he asked, "what do you want to do tonight?

"I don't know, surprise me," she told him.

"How about going to dinner and a movie."

"Sounds like a plan to me," she said with a smile of approval.

"Maybe I'll take you home and ravish you first before we do anything," Scott told her.

She laughed and asked jokingly, "Is that anything new?"

"It is every time we make love," he whispered in her ear.

"I'm happy you feel that way," she told him after they had gotten in their car and were driving out of the parking lot.

"First things first," he said as they were walking in her house. He gently picked her up and laid her on the bed and undressed her and they made love. They made love again in the shower and as they dressed Scott was watching her and he told her he was really going to miss her when she was in London.

"Yeah I'm gonna miss you too," she said.

"I'll have to make it up to you when you get home," he told her as he kissed her gently and they were leaving her house.

They picked out a good movie that this time they both enjoyed and as Scott looked at Tiffany she was dabbing her eyes with a tissue. "Are you crying?" Scott asked.

"Yeah, I am," she said. "That was a sad movie."

She was very tenderhearted about things and sometimes she left her guard down and cried easily. The two of them ordered a supreme pizza and took it back to Tiffany"s house and they had champagne as well. Tiffany no more than laid the pizza down on the counter and Scott started to undress her and she undressed him and they made love on the living room carpet first and then in bed. Afterwards Tiffany dressed in his shirt. "You look better in that thing than I do," he said smiling broadly.

"You really think so?" she asked grinning back at him as she divided up the pizza and put it on the plates.

"No, I know so," he said as he opened the bottle of champagne and poured it into the glasses.

"You have a good-looking ass," he told her as she could see her bottom when she bent over. She laughed at his comment.

As the two of them ate their pizza Tiffany's mom called and asked what she was doing and to see if she had anything new on her plate.

"No not really, Mom," she said. "Just what I told you before, that I'm leaving for London on Monday and Scott is here and we're eating pizza. I'll be in London for about a month and when I come back I'm going to work hard at getting my new store open."

"That's good," her mom said. "It sounds like things are going well for you. Well have a good weekend," her mom said, "and call me when you arrive in London."

"I will, Mom, and I hope you and Dad have a good weekend as well."

After Tiffany got off the phone Scott and her made love first on the couch and then in bed and they laid in each other's arms till morning. They made love first thing the next morning and it was almost noon when they left the house and went to the beach. They stopped at the burger hut along the way and got cheeseburgers and fries. The two of them went to the beach. They walked hand in hand up the coast and then they laid on the sand talking about everything from Tiffany going to London to her new store that she was soon to open.

"You know, Tiffany, you really make my life fun and very unpredictable," Scott told her as he kissed her. "I don't know where I'd be without you."

"I don't know where I'd be without you either," she told him.

When they got back to the house Tiffany made spaghetti and garlic bread and she made them each a salad. As they watched TV Scott undressed Tiffany and they made love first on the sofa and then in bed. Scott told Tiffany how much he loved her and they made love again before they went to sleep that night. This time Tiffany awoke first and she made pancakes and sausage and coffee. Scott came out to see what she was doing.

"Something smells delicious," he told her as he entered the kitchen. She set the plate of pancakes and sausage in front of him and he devoured his within minutes.

"I think you inhaled your breakfast this morning," she laughed.

"Yeah, I feel like it did," he told her as he patted his stomach and it was the best as usual.

"You're a very good cook," he told her.

"Yeah when I have the time and the patience," she said as she looked in his eyes. At that he took her by the hand and led her back to the bedroom and made love to her. Then they made love in the shower.

"What do you want to do today?" Scott asked as the two of them dressed.

"I would like to go shopping," she told him. "There are some things I need since I'm going away tomorrow."

"Oh! Is there now?" he asked, and she threw a pillow at him and he began tickling her.

"I'm gonna miss you something awful," he told her as he rustled her down on the bed.

"We'd better get going as this could very well lead to other things," she remarked.

"Oh, could it really?" he asked, and he added that might be a good thing.

The two of them drove to the mall and Tiffany picked up several different items. She bought a couple shirts, two pair of jeans, a dress, a pair of brown boots that came up over her knees and a very unique handbag, a leather one. It was an Italian handbag, one she really loved.

"You did really well, or at least I think you did," he told her with a sly smile.

"At least you think so!" she said smiling at him.

"The day is going by entirely too fast," Scott said looking rather sad.

Tiffany looked sad as well as they talked about going to the park for the rest of the day.

"I'll sure miss you while you're in London, baby," Scott told Tiffany while they sat arm in arm on the park bench.

"Yeah, I'm gonna miss you too," she told him.

"It's really a pretty day," Tiffany said as they watched the children at play. They walked around the park talking and confiding in one another. It was later in the day when they decided to go out to dinner. Scott decided on Mexican food. Once they got back to the house they tore each others clothes off and they made love first on the living room floor and then in bed.

"We had to make this last as we won't see each other for a month or better," Scott said. The two of them fell asleep at that.

The morning was kind of hectic as Tiffany had a ten o'clock flight to catch and Scott had to be at the agency within an hour.

"I'll see you when you get home," Scott told her as he grabbed a light jacket and headed out the door to work.

Tiffany put on a pair of white jeans and a blouse and she put on a red leather blazer as she wanted to have a professional appearance. As Tiffany boarded the plane it was crowded and she just about felt like she had been run over by the time she had taken her seat. She was jut happy to be on the plane, finally. It looked like a full flight as Tiffany watched the people board. All the people who were sitting by her were professional looking. She was sitting by a man and a woman and in front of her were two men who looked business like. Throughout the flight Tiffany read and she took a nap about halfway into the flight. As she awoke she discovered that it was starting to get dark outside. It was almost midnight when the plane landed in London.

Tiffany got off the plane and as she did she hailed a taxicab first thing. She decided to get a hotel first of all and then she went to a small sandwich shop just up the street. She didn't want to eat anything very heavy that late at night.

Once back at the hotel she was thinking about Scott and she wanted to call him and tell him she made it, but she didn't want to bother him that late at night. She went to bed that night with her mind on him and on what was in store for her throughout her time there in London.

Her first day at the studio was very interesting to say the least. She rehearsed in many scenes with actors such as Brad Pitt and actresses such as Jane Seymour. It was a very fun and interesting job and she felt she would have a good month while she was in London. It seemed like fate was smiling down on her and things were going her way. That night on her way back to the hotel she stopped at a pizza shop and ordered pizza to go and once back at the hotel she phoned Scott.

"How's everything going for you while you're in London?" Scott asked.

"Great," she told him, "but I miss you so much."

"I really miss you too," he told her.

"How are things going at the agency?" she asked.

"Busy as usual," he replied, "but there's a void where you ought to be."

She kind of laughed at his image. "I'm happy you feel that way," she told him.

"I'm gonna call my mom and see how she's doing and to let her know I arrived here and things are going well," Tiffany said.

"I'm happy to hear that all is well there with you," Scott told her.

"Well I guess I'm gonna go, but I'll talk to you tomorrow night and fill you in on anything new."

"I'm sorry you're gonna go, sweetheart," Scott said.

"I love you and I'll talk to you tomorrow night," and he made a sound that he was kissing her over the phone and she did as well to him.

Tiffany and Scott fell asleep each thinking of one another. The rest of the week went by very quickly for both Tiffany and Scott and he called on Saturday morning to see what she planned on doing over the weekend. "It's gonna be very lonely here without you," Scott remarked.

"Oh, I feel that way too, baby," she told him.

"I'm gonna go to some of the museums and do some shopping this weekend," Tiffany said.

"What's in store for you?" she asked.

"Well I'm gonna be busy today as I have a day's worth of catching up at the agency. I'm not sure about tomorrow yet," Scott replied.

"Is there anything else new?" Tiffany asked.

"Not really," he said, "but it sure is good to hear your voice."

"Yeah it's good to hear your voice too," she told him.

"Well I hate to go," he told her, "but I'm gonna have to get to the agency."

"I hate to go too," she said. Before she hung up she said, "Have a good day and I love you."

"Yes, I love you too, sweetheart," he said. "Have a good day as well. Bye, bye, baby."

"Bye, Scott," she said.

Tiffany showered and dressed for the day. She decided to wear casual attire as she got tired of dressing up and always looking her best for the camera. As she got out of the elevator and on the street she hailed a taxicab.

"Where to?" the cab driver asked.

"I think I'm gonna go to the wax museum," she told him.

She left a tip and thanked him. Once again she was in the hustle and bustle of the crowd. She went through a couple museums and she shopped at the many boutiques and the mall and by the end of the weekend she had acquired many treasures.

Sunday night before she had gone to bed the phone rang. She picked it up and Scott answered. "Hi, Babe," he said. "How's everything going in London?"

"Oh it's going well but it's very lonely," she told him.

"I can relate to that," he told her. "I want to crawl through the phone line and into your bedroom," he told her and she laughed at that image.

"I shopped till I dropped this weekend," she said.

"I'm afraid now," he told her. He could just imagine it.

"I'll have to purchase another suitcase before I come home to put everything in."

"I'm glad you had fun," he told her.

"What did you do today?" she asked.

"I spent the day at the beach," he told her. "I can hardly wait till you come home," he said.

"Well I'll talk to you real soon," she told him.

"Yeah, same here, sweetheart." At that they hung up and Tiffany went to bed with Scott on her mind and he went to bed dreaming about her.

The following week was extremely busy with photo shoots and props being set up and costume changes and the weekend went by quickly as well. Tiffany learned that she would be going home on Wednesday. She would be home that weekend. She was happy about that. She called Scott and told him she was flying home tomorrow and he was happy to hear the good news.

"I'll be here waiting with open arms," Scott told her.

As they hung up they were happy that they would be together over the weekend.

As Tiffany got off the plane back at her hometwon much to her amazement Scott was waiting for her.

"How was your trip?" he asked.

"It was good, but I'm happy to be back home in my own territory."

"I'm very happy you're back home as well," he told her.

The two of them were kissing and embracing and so happy to be in one another's arms. As Scott loaded the luggage into the car he asked, "What did you buy? Did you buy out the entire store?" he joked.

"I feel as though I did," she told him.

They chatted till they got back home and once they got in the door Scott led Tiffany to the bedroom where they made hot passionate love.

"I'm never going to let you get away from me again," he said. "Although I know it ain't going to be true." At that the two of them drifted off to sleep and Tiffany was happy to be back home and Scott was happy to have her back in his arms.

Chapter 24

When Tiffany and Scott woke up the next morning, much to their surprise they were still in each others arms, and happy to be together. They made love and Scott told Tiffany that he wanted the two of them to stay home and enjoy each other's company.

"Sounds like a wonderful idea to me," she told him.

The two of them made love several times and then again in the shower. Scott made a small breakfast and the two of them spent the day at the beach.

"This feels good now that you're back home with me," Scott said.

"I feel that way as well, baby."

Tiffany was due to open up her new store and as they lay on the beach she talked about the process.

"It'll be open by Christmas," she told Scott.

"That's great. You're an amazing woman and I'm proud of you." He added, "Keep up the good work as you're very successful. I've always said you were my star model and as fate would have it, it's true."

She was smiling up at him and he told her he would take her again if they were in the privacy of their home. At the end of the day they went out to eat and the two of them decided to spend the rest of their weekend together. It just so happened that a month later Tiffany was right. She did have her new boutique open.

Christmas was all around and Christmas music was playing in all the stores. There were Christmas trees everywhere with decorations and decorations along the street and strung across the lights. It all looked so pretty and got everyone in the Christmas spirit. All the people were scurrying along and they were bundled up as it was colder and it felt like December. Tiffany's store was doing very well and Tiffany was pleased at her success.

"You've done well, baby," Scott told her. "Good job," he added. "Life is packed full of many desire and luckily yours was fashionable as well."

www.ingramcontent.com/pod-product-compliance
Lightning Source LLC
Chambersburg PA
CBHW021552310726
48972CB00003B/791